THORNWOOD

➤ SISTERS EVER AFTER ➤

THORNWOOD

Leah Cypess

DELACORTE PRESS

Text copyright © 2020 by Leah Cypess
Jacket art copyright © 2020 by Kelsey Eng

All rights reserved. Published in the United States by Delacorte Press, an imprint of Random House Children's Books, a division of Penguin Random House LLC, New York.

Delacorte Press is a registered trademark and the colophon is a trademark of Penguin Random House LLC.

Visit us on the Web! rhcbooks.com

Educators and librarians, for a variety of teaching tools, visit us at RHTeachersLibrarians.com

Library of Congress Cataloging-in-Publication Data
Names: Cypess, Leah, author.
Title: Thornwood / Leah Cypess.
Description: New York : Delacorte Press, [2021] | Audience: Ages 9–12. |
Summary: The younger sister of Sleeping Beauty, relates how their lives have been haunted by a curse, and how she helps save the day once the curse is broken.
Identifiers: LCCN 2019060265 (print) | LCCN 2019060266 (ebook) |
ISBN 978-0-593-17883-6 (hardcover) | ISBN 978-0-593-17884-3 (library binding) |
ISBN 978-0-593-17885-0 (ebook)
Subjects: CYAC: Sisters—Fiction. | Blessing and cursing—Fiction. |
Characters in literature—Fiction.
Classification: LCC PZ7.C9972 Tho 2021 (print) | LCC PZ7.C9972 (ebook) |
DDC [Fic]—dc23

The text of this book is set in 12.5-point Golden Cockerel ITC Std.
Interior design by Carol Ly

Printed in Canada
10 9 8 7 6 5 4 3 2 1
First Edition

To Shoshana,
a sister to reckon with

➤ PROLOGUE ◄

First, let's get this out of the way: the fairy tales don't mention me. They wouldn't. The stories you've heard are all about my sister, Sleeping Beauty, with her gorgeous hair and her lovely eyes, blah blah blah. Nobody wants to hear about me, even if I was the only one who realized—right from the beginning—that the prince wasn't who he said he was.

But would any adult listen to an eleven-year-old princess who never even *got* a blessing from a fairy godmother? No.

So I'm going to tell you what really happened.

1

I've always known what would happen to my sister on her sixteenth birthday. Her doom has been hanging over her head since before I was born.

So when I woke that morning, I went straight to her room.

It was before sunrise, so Rosalin was still alone. Soon everyone would descend upon her—her ladies-in-waiting, our parents, the royal wizard. This was the day she would be struck down by her curse—the spell that, even more than her astonishing beauty, made her the center of attention everywhere she went. Today would be like every other day of her life, except a million times more intense.

And nobody but me would know how much she hated it.

From the door, my sister looked like she was still asleep, her head turned to the side and her breathing soft and even. But Rosalin is the one who taught *me* how to fake being asleep. I wasn't fooled.

I padded across the room, past delicate wooden tables piled with birthday gifts, and hopped up onto her bed.

"Hi," I said.

She didn't move. She didn't open her eyes.

"Come on," I said. "*Today,* of all days, you want to pretend to be asleep?"

Rosalin's eyes popped open, then narrowed. "That is an incredibly insensitive thing to say! What is wrong with you?" She pulled herself to a sitting position and snorted. "Aside from your hair, I mean."

I touched my hair instinctively. I hadn't brushed it before I came—not that it would have been less of a frizzy tangle if I had.

"And your face. You have chocolate on your *eyelashes*, Briony. How did you even manage that?"

She knew how I had managed it. We had sat up late last night going through her boxes of birthday chocolates, laughing and stuffing ourselves and arguing over who got the cream-filled ones.

Yet somehow, even though I hadn't left until she was nearly asleep—when I knew my plan to distract her had worked—Rosalin's face this morning was smooth and clear, unmarred by the slightest hint of exhaustion or chocolate.

"It got you up, didn't it?" I said. "We need to talk before everyone else gets here. You're going to make sure you're never alone today, right?"

Rosalin's face went tight. "Yes, Briony. I will have one of my ladies accompany me everywhere. I'm sure that's all it will take to defeat a fairy curse."

I winced. I wasn't used to hearing her refer to the curse out loud—even though everyone in the castle, everyone in the *kingdom*, knew what was supposed to happen to her today.

On the day she turns sixteen, she will prick her finger on a spinning wheel and fall asleep. She will sleep for one hundred years, and the entire castle will sleep with her. The curse will be broken only when a brave and noble prince fights his way through the thorns around the castle and wakes her with a kiss.

And that was better than her original fate. The curse the fairy queen had put on my parents, long ago, had said that their firstborn daughter would be beautiful, but would prick her finger and die on her sixteenth birthday. Rosalin's fairy godmother had managed to change the curse from *die* to *sleep for a hundred years*, which was an improvement, but still not exactly ideal.

No one knew why the fairy queen was so angry at my parents. Supposedly it was because they hadn't invited her to their wedding, but it had been decades since the fairies had attended any royal parties. According to the court minstrel, it was the fairy queen herself who had commanded that all fairies withdraw from the human world and stop meddling in human affairs. My parents had assumed inviting them was just a formality, and they hadn't gotten around to it.

And then the fairy queen had taken offense and cursed their first child.

I wanted to reach for Rosalin's hand, but the way she held herself—like her body was made of porcelain—told me she would slap me away if I tried.

"The guards have been pulling extra patrols for weeks," I said. "There's not a single spinning wheel left in the kingdom." Now I was just parroting what my father said. "You're going to be all right, Rosalin. Really."

She did her best to smile, but she didn't meet my eyes.

In my fantasies, I was always coming up with plans to save her. Ways to lift the curse and change everything. Sometimes I dreamed that I bargained with the fairy queen to place the curse solely on me and spare the rest of the castle. I imagined everyone gathered around my sleeping form, amazed at my sacrifice, while Rosalin thanked me through her tears.

I wasn't sure, deep down, that I was brave enough to sacrifice myself to save my sister. But I liked to think I was.

"Rosalin—" I began.

The door flew open, and half a dozen ladies-in-waiting poured into the room, arms full of ribbons and cloth. They fluttered around the bed, and Rosalin pasted a far more convincing smile on her face for their benefit.

Their gazes slid right past me. I pushed myself off the bed, and one of the ladies stepped on my foot.

"Ouch!" I said. She sighed heavily, annoyed that my foot had been in her way.

They gathered my sister up and swept her in the direction of the bath. I stood staring after them until she was out of sight, but Rosalin didn't look back at me even once.

I trudged back toward my room, to rouse my own ladies and convince them that I had to get ready for the party, too.

As far as I could recall, that was the last thing I did that day. That year. That century.

———◆———

The next thing I knew, I was opening my eyes and shifting uncomfortably on a cold, hard floor. I didn't remember falling asleep, but I must have; my mind felt fuzzy, and my muscles slow and sluggish, as if I hadn't moved them for . . .

. . . a hundred years.

My eyes snapped open.

The last thing I remembered was walking out of Rosalin's room, striding down the hall as the early-morning light began to filter through the windows. But now the sunlight was beating strong and bright on my face, and the floor beneath me was bare stone.

Which meant . . .

I closed my eyes again, as if I could change what I was seeing. Then, reluctantly, I opened them.

I was on the floor of a large, drafty room. In the center was a crooked wooden table with a wooden wheel perched precariously on top of it—

A spinning wheel.

"Oh, *curses*," I said.

That sort of language would have gotten me yelled at (even though it was the literal truth) if anyone else had been in the room. But no one was. I was all alone, just me and the spinning wheel.

I'm sorry, Rosalin, I thought. *I'm so sorry.*

But something was wrong. Even more wrong than the obvious.

If this had happened because of the curse, it should have been Rosalin here. Why was *I* in the room with the spinning wheel? Where was my sister?

A chill slithered up my spine. I turned my hands

over and checked all my fingertips. No blood. No sign of a prick. They were my own stubby, scratched fingers. These weren't the fingers cursed to be pricked. I had no curses hanging over my head—and no blessings, either.

I *should* have been waking up in my bed. Or in the courtyard. Or in the kitchen, or on the roof of the stables. Any of the places where I spent my time.

Instead, I was in a room I had never seen before, with a very large, very illegal spinning wheel casting a shadow on the floor.

And I couldn't remember how I had ended up here.

Fear climbed up my throat. I tried to swallow it and managed to reduce it to a churning sense of wrongness in my chest. It made it a little hard to breathe, but at least it was possible to think.

Clearly, the curse had struck. And just as clearly, it was now over. If I was awake, the prince must have come, and that meant everyone was awake. Including my sister.

I had to find her.

I got up, and my muscles creaked painfully, like I had been in the same position for hours and hours. How many hours were in a hundred years? Twenty-four hours a day multiplied by—

Not now, I told myself firmly, and started toward the door.

I wasn't sure what made me look back. Maybe a sound. Maybe an instinct. Maybe habit; I had a tendency to lose things, so I always tried to look behind me before I left a room.

There was a woman sitting at the spinning wheel.

2

The woman *definitely* had not been there a few seconds ago.

Also: she wasn't human. Her face was a bit too long, like a reflection in a warped mirror, and the tips of her ears stuck out from her silky black hair. Her eyes were large and angled, yellow like a cat's. A pair of wings was folded flat against her back.

A fairy.

"Princess Briony," she said. As she spoke, she began to spin. The wheel whirred as she pedaled, and her fingers fed lumps of wool into the spinning bobbin. "You are not who I was expecting."

Her voice was low and mocking. Like I was *exactly* who she had been expecting and there was something funny about that.

"Who are you?" I demanded, shrinking back. "Are you the fairy who cursed my sister?"

The fairy snorted, still spinning. "Of course not. Do I *look* like the fairy queen to you?"

Since she was the first fairy I had ever seen, I had no answer for that.

The wool lumps were dingy when she fed them in, but gleamed like gold when they came out. The fairy looked at me, her feet still working the pedals. "I'm your sister's fairy godmother. I'm the one who *saved* her."

Not that she had done a very good job of it. Turning "prick her finger and die" into "prick her finger and fall asleep" was, admittedly, an improvement. But it wasn't as good as, say, "Prick her finger and turn everything she touches to gold," or, "Prick her finger and sneeze," or, you know, "Prick her finger and nothing will happen, enjoy your sixteenth birthday, Rosalin!"

But I wasn't about to bring that up. The court minstrel said ordinary fairies didn't have enough power to cancel a curse set by their queen. He also said they were sensitive about that subject.

"If you're Rosalin's fairy godmother," I said suspiciously, "shouldn't you be helping her?"

"Maybe that's what I'm doing," the fairy said.

She didn't particularly emphasize the *maybe*. But I noticed it.

I focused on what was important. "Where's Rosalin?"

The fairy smiled. Her teeth were too small for her

mouth, and there were too many of them. "That's the question, isn't it?"

"Yes," I said. "That's the question. What's the answer? I need to make sure she's all right."

"Do you?" She spread her wings. They were long and gossamer, like a dragonfly's. "Maybe you should worry about yourself instead of running after your sister. Maybe today you're the important one."

It was like she had reached right into my heart and pulled out my deepest, most secret wish. Fairies are good at that.

But they're also tricky, and dangerous. And good at distraction.

"My sister," I said again. "Where is she?"

The fairy's fingers went still, and the wheel came to a stop. There was already a thick coil of gold thread wound around the bobbin.

"Too late," she said. "The one who calls himself a prince has already found her."

She snarled slightly on the word *prince*, like she meant something else entirely.

"Obviously the prince found her," I said. "He found her, he kissed her, that's why we all woke up. But where *is* she?"

"Come here," the fairy said. "Spin some thread for me. While you do, I will tell you where your sister is."

I didn't hesitate.

"Sorry," I said. "That doesn't sound like a good idea. I'll go find her myself."

"You might not like what you find," the fairy warned.

I turned and walked out of the room without responding.

The door opened onto a landing, the top of a curved stairway. The stairs went steeply downward, curving around and around a slick stone pillar. There were three narrow windows set high in the outer walls, but the light that filtered through them was weak and dusty.

I don't like heights. I took a deep breath, put one hand on the damp stone, and started down,

down,

down,

down,

down.

My knees creaked like I was an old woman, or like I hadn't moved them in years. Both, I supposed, were sort of true.

But as I descended the stairs, my legs warmed up, and I started feeling more like myself. Aside from the stiffness in my muscles, it felt like I had been asleep for no more than a night. There was no dust in my clothes, there were no cobwebs on the stairs, and my nails were trim—they had been cut for Rosalin's party.

I let a small part of myself believe that only a single day had passed. That made it easier to stay calm as I trudged down the stairs toward whatever waited for me.

I hadn't known our castle had towers this high. And I couldn't tell how much farther I had to go. The stairs circled the pillar so tightly that I couldn't see more than six or seven steps below me. I also couldn't hear anything. Not a sound.

The one who calls himself a prince has already found her.

The fairy had said it like it had *just* happened. And she hadn't said he'd kissed her. What if he hadn't? What if Rosalin hadn't woken?

If she hadn't, nobody had. That was how the curse worked.

What if it was so silent because I was the only person in the castle who was awake?

A shiver ran up my legs, and suddenly they were too rubbery to hold me up. I stopped walking and leaned against the outer wall. The stone was cold and rough, and a jagged bit of rock dug between my shoulder blades.

I pushed down my rising terror. *Don't panic*, I told myself. *It won't help.*

We can deal with this. That was what my father, the king, used to say every time the curse came up. *We can stop it.*

I had never really believed him. I don't think he even believed himself.

One last breath, and I pushed away from the wall and kept going down the stairs, around and around. I started feeling dizzy, and the muscles in my legs burned, but oddly, I had no trouble going forward. It was like my body was trying to tell me I was tired, but I wasn't *actually* tired.

My head was spinning when I finally reached the bottom. The stairway ended at a door, thick and solid and very, very shut.

And locked? Was I locked into this tower, with the spinning wheel and the fairy godmother?

Don't panic. I put both hands on the door and pushed with all my might. It swung open so hard it slammed into the wall behind it, then rebounded with so much force that I had to use both hands to catch it.

Okay, then. Not locked.

Once the echoes of the slam faded, everything went back to being silent. The hallway stretching in front of me was empty.

Nobody was coming to check on that bang? The castle was *crawling* with busybodies. Once, I'd accidentally dropped a frog into an empty suit of armor (long story), and within seconds, a dozen people were running at me wanting to know what was going on. And now, no one?

My sense of unease crept higher.

I looked over my shoulder. The stairs stretched up, up,

and up to that room with the spinning wheel. Ahead of me, the hallway was long and narrow and deathly quiet. Not just because there was no sound. It was more like sound had ceased to exist. Like noise wasn't even possible.

"Aaaah," I said experimentally. My voice sounded tiny and insignificant and was quickly swallowed by the unnatural hush.

I wouldn't try that again. The silence was better.

I carefully closed the door behind me. Then I walked down the hall.

I'd like to say I was being brave. If this story was about me, I guess that's what it *would* say.

But the truth is, I couldn't think of anything else to do.

3

I got to my sister's room just in time to see the prince lean down and kiss her.

I kind of wish I had gotten there thirty seconds later.

It could have been worse. It wasn't a *gross* kiss. Just a peck on the lips—polite and distant—and then the prince straightened and stepped back from the bed.

My sister lay unmoving, her eyes closed. Her hair fell in waves around her long lavender gown. (Rosalin always wore gowns, even to study Latin or go riding.) Her face was perfect, her features exquisite, her skin glowing.

I was used to all that. Judging by his rapt expression, the prince was not.

He was pretty good-looking himself. His clothes were surprisingly shabby, and ripped in various places, but he was tall and angular, with thick black hair. I couldn't tell what color his eyes were, since he hadn't bothered to look at me yet, but I hoped they were blue. Flashing, dazzling blue. Rosalin had a thing for blue eyes. After all she had gone through, she deserved that, at least.

"My princess," he said, which seemed a bit—forward? Presumptuous? Not really, I guess; he *had* just rescued her from an evil spell.

Rosalin opened her eyes, a slow flutter of lashes. She looked at the prince and smiled.

He put his hand on his heart and dropped to one knee.

I think that was the moment I decided I hated him.

Honestly! Who kisses a girl they haven't even met? And yes, I know, there was a spell, it was a curse; obviously Rosalin would rather be kissed by a stranger than sleep for the rest of her life. It was the fairy's fault, not the prince's.

But I have to say, he didn't look as if he felt the slightest bit guilty about it.

Rosalin struggled to sit up, her lips still curved in a smile. Then she turned her head and saw me.

An expression of absolute terror passed over her face.

Just for a second, and then it was gone. So fast I wasn't sure I had seen it.

I must have imagined it. It didn't make sense; no one was ever scared of me. No one noticed me at all. Usually, when ambassadors from other countries came to the castle, they were surprised to see me. No one had bothered to tell them I existed.

You might think that would upset me, but I was used to it. It was the way things had always been. Rosalin was the older princess, *and* she was astonishingly beautiful, *and* she was the victim of a tragic fairy curse. People always wanted to look at her, and hear about her, and say they had met her.

I wasn't jealous. Well, I mostly wasn't jealous. The lack of attention left me free to explore the castle and the gardens, which was a lot more fun than entertaining ambassadors.

Besides, we had very few ambassadors. My father kept pressing other princes to propose to Rosalin, and it made people avoid us. While it was true that she was at the age when most princesses would be getting engaged, nobody was interested, because everyone knew what would happen to her on her sixteenth birthday. Aside from the fact that it made an engagement pointless, whoever was engaged to her would be *obligated* to try to fight his way into the castle and wake her with a kiss. None of our neighboring countries were willing to risk their princes.

A couple of weeks earlier—well, a couple of weeks as I remembered it—a dukedom had sent their sixth son, whom I guess they could spare, to court Rosalin. Unfortunately, he was twelve years old, so she hadn't taken him seriously. He and I had a fun time—it turned out he was fond of climbing on rooftops, just like me—and for the first time ever, I knew what it felt like to have a friend. I could say whatever I wanted around him, without thinking about whether I would be laughed at.

It lasted until Rosalin announced that she was formally rejecting his offer of marriage and he was sent home. I didn't speak to my sister for two days afterward, and we finally had it out in a huge fight. She told me she wasn't going to "string anyone along" and she wouldn't settle for anything less than a true and noble prince who was an actual adult. I shouted that maybe she should think about what *I* wanted for once, instead of everything always being about her. Then I threw a wooden bowl at her face. She caught it and threw it back, and after ten minutes of back-and-forth, we were laughing. I laughed so hard I cried.

But no one was laughing now. Rosalin went on looking at me, her face blank, until the prince cleared his throat. Then we both looked at him.

"My lady," he said. He *did* have blue eyes, though they were pale, not particularly dazzling. "You have been asleep for a long time."

"Um, yeah," I said. "We knew that."

Rosalin shot me a glare and got out of bed. *Her* muscles didn't creak; she rose to her feet as gracefully as if she'd been practicing the move for the past hundred years.

"My prince," she said.

He rose and bowed. "Prince Varian of Glenall, a kingdom across the northern sea. I heard of your plight and of your beauty and have traveled many leagues to save you. I fought my way to the castle—"

"Fought *who?*" I asked.

"Briony," Rosalin hissed. *"Go away."*

My shoulders stiffened. I had come straight to her room to make sure she was all right. She had no business acting like I was irrelevant just because some prince had gotten here first.

"I have just as much right to be here as you do," I said.

"No, you don't. It's my room. Go back to yours. And change your dress while you're at it. Did you not notice that stain?"

I forced myself not to look down. "Who," I said to the prince, "did you have to fight?"

The prince looked at me. His expression was kind and gentle and a little pitying. People often looked at me like that when I was in the same room as Rosalin. "Ever since you fell asleep, a forest of thorns has guarded your castle against any who would harm you, but it has also blocked it from any who would save you. Everyone knew that breaking the spell would make the Thornwood vanish, but someone had to get through it first. Dozens of princes have tried, and they all came away bloodied and beaten."

Rosalin's eyelashes swept upward. "Until you."

"Right time, right place," I said. "Good move."

Rosalin shot me a glare. "Ignore my sister. At her christening, she was given the gift of being the most annoying of them all."

"That's not true!" I snapped. "I never even had a christening! Guess why?"

The prince looked confused.

Rosalin flicked her fingers at me dismissively. "That's right," she said. "No beauty, no brilliance, no charm for her. In case you hadn't noticed."

"Your fairy godmother," I said, "never said anything about brilliance or charm. In case *you* hadn't noticed."

Rosalin turned back to Prince Varian. "How *did* you manage to get to me?"

He looked relieved to have a question he knew the answer to. "I had a magic sword."

Of course he did.

"It took hours. Every time I cut through the branches, they grew back. Toward the end, they wrapped themselves around my blade and wrested it from me. It vanished within the thorns before I had time to even grab for it." He shuddered. "I admit, my lady, I almost despaired. But I thought of you, trapped in your slumber, and I knew I could not give up. I fought my way through the last few yards with my bare hands." He held his arms out, palms up. His hands and forearms were covered with bloody scratches.

I have to admit, I was impressed. Even if I couldn't help noticing that somehow, even though his arms and hands were all scraped up, not a single scratch marred his much-too-handsome face.

Rosalin gazed up at him, looking like she was going to swoon.

I shivered. "Where did you get a magic sword?"

Prince Varian was too busy staring into Rosalin's eyes to answer. I wasn't sure either of them had even heard the question.

Something sharp went through my chest. I tried to ignore it, to be happy for Rosalin. She had been through so much, living her life under the shadow of a curse. Now it was over. We all had our freedom. She had her prince.

And she didn't need me anymore.

I walked past the pair, who were now leaning so far toward each other I suspected they were both about to fall flat on their faces—*be happy for her, be happy for her*—and headed for the large windows on the far side of Rosalin's room. They faced south, which meant the village was right across from them.

If there still was a village. Most of the people who lived there had worked in the castle. Why would they stick around once they couldn't *get* to work anymore? And who would want to live near a castle under an evil curse?

Suddenly I wasn't sure I wanted to look out. But I forced myself to walk to the windows, which were wide open and framed by gold-trimmed curtains of white velvet. I put my elbows on the windowsill and pushed the curtains aside.

But I couldn't see whether the village was still there.

We were on the top floor, but I couldn't see anything at all. The window was entirely covered by a tangle of thick dark branches bristling with thorns.

4

I let out a shriek and stepped back from the window. My arm hit the curtain, knocking it over the windowsill and into the thorns.

The branches twisted and grabbed the curtain, pouncing as if they were alive. They dug their sharp points into the thick fabric, and the velvet tore with a jagged sound, so violently that it was ripped free of the curtain rod. The curtain fell and vanished, swallowed by the thorns.

One vine straightened, a wisp of shredded fabric dangling from its end. It shot upward and grazed the underside of my wrist. I snatched my hand away.

"Rosalin?" I said. My voice came out shrill.

Rosalin was at my side instantly. We looked at the bristling, hungry thorns covering the window.

"Don't be afraid," the prince said behind us.

Sure. That was useful advice.

I stepped away from him. My skin felt too tight. When

Prince Varian put one hand on Rosalin's shoulder, my arm muscles tensed.

I didn't know what it was about him that rubbed me the wrong way. But *something* wasn't right.

"The Thornwood should be gone now that the spell is broken," Rosalin said. Her voice was high and thin. "Why is it still here?"

I reached for her hand, but she was already shrinking against Varian's side, looking up at him with wide trusting eyes.

"It *will* be gone," Varian said. He reached out somewhat hesitantly and put his arm around Rosalin. When she buried her face in his shoulder, he let out a breath and pulled her close. "The spell is broken. The Thornwood will fade away. I'm sure of it."

"Does it *look* like it's fading?" I said. Outside the window, a broken branch scraped against the windowsill, a scrap of white velvet clinging to its tip. "Don't the stories say it will disappear once you cut your way through it? Or at least once you kiss Rosalin? Something is wrong."

Varian looked over Rosalin's head at me. His eyes were troubled, in contradiction to his reassuring tone. "There are dozens of stories. They don't all agree. And they're obviously not complete. I mean ..." He gave me an apologetic look. "None of them mentions you."

I did my best to look like I didn't care.

"In the town," Varian admitted, "they did believe the Thornwood would disappear as soon as the spell was broken."

I straightened. "The town? You mean the village? It's still there?"

"Oh, yes," Varian said. "It's grown quite large."

I bit my lip on a small smile. I loved the village, even though I didn't get to go there very often. I'd once had a governess who was being courted by the village tailor, and she had snuck me over a few times, disguising me as common girl. I'd been able to run around the square, barefoot and dirty. I had learned how to play dice. It was the most fun I'd ever had in my life.

I wasn't sure why it felt so important that the village was still there. The people in it, the other children I had played with, even my governess, would be dead by now. But it was good to know there *were* people out there, beyond the forest of thorns, who knew about us and what had happened to us.

"But if the castle is surrounded by thorns," Rosalin said, pulling away from him, "what do the people in the village *do*?"

Varian shrugged. "There are princes who come there, to try to fight their way through the Thornwood and wake the beautiful princess sleeping in the castle. They need places to sleep, stables for their horses, and all that. Then, after they fail, they generally need new weapons. And new clothes. And lots of ale . . ."

"That's what the villagers do now?" Rosalin looked like she wasn't sure whether to be delighted or horrified. "They provide services for heroes?"

"Partly. There aren't as many heroes as you might think. But there are a lot of ordinary people who want to see the Thornwood. Every fall there's a big ceremony when people throw items into the Thornwood and watch them get torn to bits. They say it's very helpful for those trying to get rid of bad memories. Visitors come from all over. And in the summer, there's a music festival. . . ." He stopped, finally noticing that Rosalin had settled on horrified. "Um. Maybe when we get out of here, I'll take you to it. They have some very nice songs about you."

"Can we focus on the part where we get out of here?" I said. "Do you have any heroic plans for accomplishing *that?*"

It came out nasty—even I could hear it. But that was the only way I could keep my voice from trembling. The fear had lodged in my throat, and it wasn't going away.

Because the magic sword—the one Varian had used to get to us—was gone. Which meant we had no way to get through the Thornwood.

If we were trapped within the walls of this castle, what was the point of waking up? Just so we could all die when our food ran out?

Varian didn't seem to notice my tone. "I'll find a way," he said. To Rosalin, not to me. "Even if I have to fight my way through the entire forest. I won't let anything happen to you."

"That's brave," I said. "But it doesn't seem very practical. We need to find our parents and tell them—"

Neither of them was listening to me. Rosalin looked up at the prince, her eyes wide and her lashes trembling. He pulled her closer.

The door to the room burst open, and half a dozen ladies-in-waiting spilled in.

Varian and Rosalin jumped apart. I wasn't sure why. It wasn't a secret to anyone that there had been kissing going on in this room.

"Your Highness!"

"What happened?"

"Are you all right?"

"Did . . . did the curse . . ."

They descended on Rosalin and the prince in a flurry of colorful silk and strong perfume. They weren't all *Rosalin's* ladies-in-waiting—two of them were mine—but not one of them glanced at me.

Which gave me a chance to slip out of the room.

This isn't what's supposed to happen.

I hurried down the corridor, my mind whirling. The spell was finally broken. The prince had saved us. We were supposed to be safe. We were supposed to be *free*.

Something had gone terribly wrong. But what?

Whatever it was, it couldn't have happened while we were asleep. It must have happened either after we woke or before the spell struck. If I could just remember . . .

"Watch it!" a familiar voice shouted, and I had just enough time to jerk my head up before I slammed into someone running along the corridor toward my sister's room.

We both landed on the floor. I skidded across the rug and hit my head on the tapestry-covered wall.

The other person got it even worse. He had been carrying a lute, and he clutched it to his chest as he fell, protecting the instrument rather than himself. As a result, he slammed down flat on his back. The thud made me wince despite my own pain.

"I'm sorry!" I gasped, scrambling to my feet. I recognized the person I had bumped into: the court minstrel, dressed all in black, clutching his polished wooden lute.

I wasn't surprised that he was here: he was obsessed with Rosalin's legend, and convinced that the songs he wrote about it would make him famous. Rosalin was the sole reason he had accepted a post in my father's castle. It wasn't like we had enough money to afford his usual salary.

"Are you all right?" I said.

There was no answer, which confirmed my fear: he must have been knocked out cold. The only time the court minstrel was *ever* silent was when he was unconscious.

A moment later, though, he groaned and sat up. He peered at his lute, running his hand over the neck and strings to make sure they were intact. Only then did he look at me. "Princess Briony! Your parents are terribly worried about you and your sister."

"I'll go find them," I said quickly. The last thing I needed was for him to run back to my parents and report on my whereabouts.

"Good, good." He got to his feet. He was wearing black hose, a long black cape, and a black bandanna around his forehead with a black feather sticking out of it. (Why a feather? Who knew? It wasn't even the kind of feather you would use for a quill.) "Where is your beautiful sister?"

"Um," I said. Rosalin hated the minstrel, who never tired of writing songs about how doomed and tragic she was. "She's . . . busy."

Wrong answer. His eyes lit up. "With her brave and handsome prince?"

"Uh ..."

"I must find them." The minstrel swept his cape behind him. "I have already started writing my song about her awakening, and I need to talk to everyone of importance so I can get the details right." He strummed his lute. "Finally, the time has come for me to perfect my masterpiece. Do you want to hear the first stanza?"

"Not real—"

"The sleeping beauty rests abed," he sang, his voice soaring and dipping. *"Though all the birds and beasts have fled. Her ladies slumber at her side, all punished for a fairy's pride!"*

The minstrel did have a beautiful voice. My mother often encouraged him to use it to sing songs that other people had written.

"I'm going to call it 'Sleeping Beauty,'" he said, lowering his lute. "What do you think?"

I thought it was a ridiculous title. I would have said so if yet another lady-in-waiting hadn't rushed by us at that moment, her face streaked with tears. She pulled open the door to Rosalin's room, and we all heard my sister say, "Yes, I know they're worried, but I can't leave this room without changing! I've been wearing the same gown for a hundred years!"

The minstrel rushed past me toward the room. The lady-in-waiting glanced at him, stepped swiftly inside, and shut the door.

"Princess!" the minstrel cried. He pounded on the door. "It is I! I must have the chance to gaze once more upon your beauty, now that we are all saved! I must hear how it happened and speak to your prince! Let me in!"

Part of me wanted to stay and see how that worked out for him.

But of course, what the minstrel didn't know—yet—was that we *weren't* saved. If anything, we were in worse danger than ever. At least with Rosalin's enchanted slumber, the fairy had told us how the spell would end. Now that the spell *had* ended, we knew nothing about what would happen next.

The minstrel cleared his throat and began to sing. "*He woke the princess fair. Then she felt sunlight on her hair.* But *does* the sunlight shine on your bed? Let me in, Princess! Let me in so I can check my facts!"

I turned my back on my sister's room and headed down the hall while behind me, the minstrel's voice faded into the distance.

5

Going unnoticed is one of my most valuable talents, and I put it to good use as I made my way through the castle, searching for my parents.

They had apparently already checked my room. So not only were they worried about me, they probably thought it was my fault that they were worried.

My parents loved me, but I knew they also found me difficult. (I knew because they often said, *Briony, why do you have to be so difficult?*) When I was born, they had been hoping they would get another beautiful, graceful daughter, only this time without the nasty curse hanging over her head.

Instead, they got me.

My parents tried. They didn't have much time to spend with me—they had a kingdom to run and a spinning wheel ban to enforce—but despite our financial constraints, they spared no expense when it came to my governesses or my tutors. (Or my hairdressers.) They threw huge birthday parties for me and bought me magnificent presents. But they never seemed to know what to say to me. Once they determined that I was in good health and hadn't gotten into any serious trouble, they usually fell back on reminiscing about puppet shows I had loved when I was five years old.

But they were good monarchs, even if they weren't amazing parents. Once I found them and they knew I was all right, I would tell them about the Thornwood, and they would . . .

I couldn't finish the thought. I didn't really believe they would know what to do. When it came to fairy curses, there usually wasn't much humans *could* do. And it wasn't like my parents had been able to save us the first time around.

Still. They commanded the king's guard: over a dozen highly trained men with a whole armory of swords. Surely if all those men worked together, they could cut down the Thornwood.

On the other hand, if ordinary men with ordinary swords could cut through the Thornwood, wouldn't the villagers have done it by now?

My parents will know what to do. I clung to the thought.

Even if I didn't fully believe it, I believed it enough to keep myself from panicking.

I passed three people on my way toward the stairs: a squire, the housekeeper, and a chambermaid. Even so, as I crept through the corridors of the second floor, the castle seemed a lot emptier than I remembered.

Before the curse, I couldn't walk down a hallway without passing several visiting nobles, two or three maids bearing trays of delicious-smelling food, a self-important page or two carrying a rolled-up letter, and the ever-present and always-silent servants whose job it was to keep everything spotless. I wouldn't even have noticed any of them; they were practically part of the background. I would only pay attention to those who affected me: a new hairdresser (Rosalin went through them like handkerchiefs, and the new ones always thought they would be the one to finally fix my hair), one of my tutors, or the permanently grouchy royal gardener, who'd had it in for me ever since the time my pet canary got into her flower seeds.

Now, though, the hallways were almost empty. The rug-covered floors, the walls with their somber tapestries, the narrow polished wooden benches—all were silent, making my footsteps sound louder and louder as I walked faster and faster.

Where *was* everyone?

I started opening doors as I went, glancing into bed-rooms. Every last one was empty and neatly packed away. Why?

When I reached the corridor that branched toward my room, I hesitated, then turned sharply left and hur-ried down the hallway. I wanted to check on Twirtle, my canary. He would surely be fine—he was a bird; he would have no way of knowing he had slept longer than a single night—but I wanted to make sure. I wanted to lift him onto my finger, have him cock his head at me and chirp. He was a plain little thing, dull yellow with non-descript brown markings, but when he sang, the chirps and trills filled my room with music. Sometimes I could get him to perch on my shoulder while he sang.

I was smiling as I pushed open the door to my room. I felt the stretch in my cheeks, like my skin was crack-ing, and realized that this was the first time I had truly smiled since I woke up.

My room was only a bit smaller than Rosalin's, and my furniture was just as ornate as hers—though I had a tendency to leave my clothes draped over everything, which gave a less elegant impression. My nightdress was still crumpled on my dresser, along with several pages of math and history lessons, and three pairs of shoes were strewn across the floor. I ignored all that, heading straight for the large golden cage near the far wall, with its dangling maple leaves and grape clusters and gold-embroidered cover and—

—and its open door.

I heard a cry, and didn't realize it was my own until I stumbled across the room and the cry came with me.

The golden door swayed slightly on its hinges. The cage was empty. Well, not *empty*—Twirtle's silver perches were there, and his gilded bath was full of water. But there was no small yellow bird, no flutter of feathers as he hopped down to his food container.

How could this be? The castle had been frozen in time during the spell, which meant there had been no one awake to open the cage. And even if someone had opened it, Twirtle would have been asleep. . . .

I felt a draft of cool air on the back of my neck and realized that my window was open.

I started toward it, then stopped short. Thorn branches filled the window, a solid, gnarled, deadly wall. Twirtle couldn't have gotten out that way.

But he might have tried, and . . .

Bile rose in my throat, thick and sour. I swallowed it and forced myself to walk to the window, braced for the sight of yellow feathers caught in those cruel thorns.

No, I thought. *No, no, please no* . . .

Tears filled my eyes when I reached the window.

But there was no hint of yellow—of any bright color at all—in the gnarled brown branches.

I let my breath out in a choked gasp. Twirtle hadn't gone out the window. Of course he hadn't. He was too smart for that. He was in this castle somewhere, flying around, looking for me. Well, more likely looking for food. He had escaped before—most memorably, that time when the gardener had caught him. I just had to find him.

A long, slow hiss sounded from the window, like rough branches sliding against each other. I stepped back quickly and blinked the tears from my eyes.

Twirtle was probably in the kitchen. After all, that was where the food was. If he wasn't there—or in the gardener's workshop—then my parents would assign a maid to search for him. They had done it before, when they'd seen how upset I was.

Guilt niggled at me. I knew I should go to my parents first; they must be frantic by now. But they were probably in the royal sitting room, and the kitchen was practically on the way there. One quick stop wouldn't hurt.

I headed determinedly for the door but paused next to my gold-framed mirror. I swiped the wetness from my lashes, then examined myself carefully, looking for signs that I was a hundred years older.

Rosalin was right—there was a stain on my dress. But I wasn't sure how she had even noticed it, given the state of my hair. It was no longer than it had been a hundred years ago. It *had*, however, been flattened on one side while I slept, but only enough to keep it from standing straight out from my head, which was what it was doing on the other side.

Rosalin is prettier than me in every way, but the only thing I envy her is her hair. She has smooth, sleek, shiny black hair that glimmers like a waterfall every time she moves. If she does nothing to it, it falls straight and neat down her back. If she puts it up in braids, it behaves perfectly, making her look elegant and poised.

My hair is a color that's hard to describe ("like mud that's been stirred with bathwater" is how Rosalin once put it), and if I do nothing to it, it looks like "a mass of frizz that's been hit by a lightning bolt" (also Rosalin). If I do something to it, it looks like a mass of frizz with some ribbons buried inside.

When I was eight years old, I hacked off my hair with a knife. I thought it would form a smooth cap around my head and I would look fierce and intimidating. That would be *better* than beautiful.

Instead, without any weight to hold it down, my hair was "free to do its worst." (Rosalin again. On the subject of my hair, she was practically a poet.) My parents wouldn't let me leave the castle until the ball of frizz around my head had grown long enough to be tied back. By the time it did, I felt like I wanted to tear every strand out by its roots.

And now I was going to be trapped within these walls for a lot longer than that.

Or maybe a lot less. Depending on how much food and water we had.

The thought of food made my stomach rumble, which strengthened my decision to go to the kitchen. I smoothed the front of my dress and pushed my hair back from my face. I knew that if I looked in the mirror again, I would see doubt written all over my tear-streaked face.

So I didn't look. I lifted my chin and headed out the door.

6

The kitchen was deserted.

The oven was unlit, and baskets were stacked neatly on the shelves. Pots hung clean and shiny from the ceiling near the walls. On the table sat a tower of cake, white and pink and silver layers, with an elaborate design of flowers coiling around its side.

Rosalin's sixteenth-birthday cake. Frozen in time, just like everything else in the castle.

There had been some fuss over this cake. The pastry chef had refused to make it on the day of Rosalin's party, as my mother had ordered. He had insisted on making it early, and then it had been so big there was nowhere to keep it, and the cook had insisted that it was in her way "and blocks my view and is going to topple over at any second!" There had been a fight between them, which had resulted in the cook "accidentally" mixing cumin into the cinnamon right before the chef baked five dozen trays of cinnamon cookies.

My mother had said it was a bad idea to have a celebration in the first place. Everyone knew that the fairy curse was supposed to take effect on Rosalin's sixteenth birthday. "It would be best," my mother had said, "for us to pass the day in quiet watchfulness."

My father had disagreed.

"There is not a single spinning wheel in our kingdom. Rosalin is safe. We are celebrating not just our daughter's birthday, but our triumph over the curse."

His voice, deep and rumbly, was clear in my mind. It was one of the few clear things. My memories felt murky, like I was seeing them from underwater. And no wonder: a hundred years had passed since the chef had fought with the cook and my father made his boast. I hadn't grown or changed for one second of those hundred years. The cake looked as fresh and moist as if it had been baked yesterday. But my mind somehow sensed that everything I remembered was ancient news. That around us, outside this castle, *everything* had changed.

All because of Rosalin and her stupid curse. My life had always revolved around her. And the curse wasn't over: we were still trapped; we still had to be afraid. All because of *her* spell. She'd gone and pricked her finger on a spinning wheel, despite knowing her *entire life* that she shouldn't go anywhere near a spinning wheel, and now everything was ruined and she didn't even care.

Ignore my sister. Easy for Rosalin to say, when she knew that everyone *would*. That she would still be the center of everything, the one everyone tried to protect, even though our entire situation was her fault to begin with.

I crossed the empty kitchen to the cake. Sugar crunched under my feet. The cake smelled like buttercream with a tinge of lemon. The frosting coiled in delicate spirals, with roses so realistic that there were fake drops of sugared dew on their petals. It really was a masterpiece.

A pointless masterpiece. We had nothing to celebrate.

I plucked a rose off the side of the cake and bit into it. It was thin and brittle, with a sugary crunch. I swallowed it whole, then plunged my hand into the side of the middle tier, through the elegant whirls of frosting, and came out with a fistful of moist yellow cake. I stuffed it into my mouth and reached for another.

The first chunk was delicious, an explosion of richness in my mouth. It was even slightly warm, like it had recently come out of the oven. The second chunk tasted salty. That was when I realized I was crying.

I reached for another handful of cake, but instead of eating it, I threw it across the room. It splattered against a clay jug and slid slowly to the floor.

"Whoa," someone said.

I spun around.

A boy I had never seen before stood in the kitchen doorway. His eyes were wide and his face was dirty. His brown hair was slightly shaggy. His face, his hair, and his clothes were liberally dusted with flour. He must have been one of the kitchen boys.

I felt a blush creep up my face and shook the remnants of cake off my hand. Crumbs scattered on the floor, but the frosting stuck to my fingers.

"Sorry," the boy said. His mouth was curved up on one side, like he was trying not to laugh. "I didn't mean to interrupt you."

I was almost happy that he was making fun of me. Anger felt better than embarrassment. "You're not interrupting me. I'm done."

"Really?" he said. "Aren't you going to topple the cake?"

I *had* been about to do that, though I hadn't realized it until he said it. I responded in my haughtiest voice. "Certainly not."

"Of course not," he agreed. "Then you would have to bend down to throw more of it across the room. That would be undignified."

When the kitchen girls laughed at me—for the stains on my clothes, or the tangles in my hair, or my histrionic rages when Rosalin and I fought—they would do it behind my back. It was brave of this boy, I supposed, to laugh to my face.

"Excuse me," I said, lifting my chin. "I must go."

"If you *do* want to topple the cake, I'll help you."

"I think I can handle it by myself. If I was going to handle it. Which I wasn't."

The boy studied the cake. "Are you sure? It seems like it would make you feel better."

"Maybe," I said. "But it won't change anything, will it?"

"It might change how you feel."

There were still tears trickling down the sides of my nose, but I couldn't wipe them off without smearing frosting all over my face. I looked around. No towel in sight.

"Have you seen a canary, by any chance?" I said.

The boy blinked. "No."

"Where are the kitchen maids?" I demanded. "Estella, and Greta, and Siobel—"

The boy looked uncomfortable. "I don't think they're here."

"I can see that."

"I mean, they're not anywhere in the castle."

"Where else would they be?"

He looked at me like I was dimwitted. "No one who

lives in the village came to work this morning. I mean, that morning. They didn't want to get stuck here when the curse . . . you know."

That was why the pastry chef hadn't wanted to bake the cake on Rosalin's birthday. He wasn't planning to be here. No one was planning to be here, unless they had nowhere else to be.

I tried to reach into my fuzzy memories, to see if the kitchen girls had told me what they were going to do. Nope. They hadn't said a word.

Well. I had always known they weren't really my friends, that they had to pretend they liked me because I was a princess. But a tiny, secret part of me had never stopped hoping they liked me for real.

So much for that.

"They must be dead by now," the boy added. "Everyone we know must be dead, unless they're in the castle with us." He bit the side of his lip, as if trying not to laugh out loud.

Hysteria, I thought. But that wasn't it. There was a smug note in his voice, as if he was sincerely delighted by the thought of all those people being dead.

My fingernails dug into my palms. "Before you get too triumphant about it," I said, "you should realize that the castle isn't the safest place to be right now, either. Have you looked out a window since you woke?"

He pursed his lips. "I have."

"And the view doesn't worry you?"

"The prince is here. He can cut us out, can't he?"

"Not without his sword," I said. "Which, apparently, he left in the Thornwood."

"Did he?" The boy's eyes narrowed. "How careless of him."

Why was I trying to frighten a random servant? Just because I was scared didn't mean everyone else had to be. "It's all right," I said. "We'll figure out a solution, don't worry. I'm working on it right now." Though "working on it" was admittedly a bit of an exaggeration. "Do you know where the king and queen are?"

I was talking to empty air. The boy was running out the kitchen door.

I wiped my hands clean on the side of the table— the cook, after all, wasn't here to yell at me for it—and looked again at the cake. There was now an ugly hollow in its side, with yellow crumbs and bits of frosting jumbled together inside it.

I thought about pushing it over, but that no longer seemed worth the effort. What did it matter whose fault it was that we were trapped in here? What mattered was getting *out*.

I had to find my parents.

I headed for the royal sitting room, taking the servants'

way because it was quicker. That turned out to be a mistake. I had only gone this way once or twice, and my memories were vague and incomplete. Somehow, when I got to the turn I thought led to the sitting room, I found myself facing a long hallway ending at a large bay window with thorn branches pressed against it.

The hall was deserted, its walls bare stone—it had become too expensive to repair tapestries once we'd stopped spinning our own thread—and the thorn-covered window didn't let in much light. The shadows seemed darker and sharper than shadows should be. I shivered, then forced myself to walk to the end of the hall. If I could just figure out which side of the castle I was on . . .

But the view from the window didn't help me. The thorns were a thick bramble, letting only the faintest bits of sunlight through. Still, there *was* sunlight, and the sunlight in the tower had been coming from the east. So I was probably facing east now. Which meant that to get to the throne room, I had to turn—

Something snapped around my wrist, driving sharp spikes into my skin.

I screamed and yanked my arm. The branch that had grabbed me yanked back so hard that I was dragged toward the window.

"No!" My voice split the silence. "Let go!" I tried to dig my heels in, but I was no match for the strength of the branch pulling me. "Help! Someone, help!"

There was no answer but the relentless sound of my heels slowly being dragged along the rug.

7

The branch pulled, slowly and steadily. Thorns dug into my wrist with sharp stabs of fiery pain. I pulled back with all my strength, and agony shot through my arm. With my free hand, I reached out frantically for something to hold on to. My fingers closed on empty air.

My feet hit the wall below the window. Another branch snaked along the sill and tangled in my hair. A third coiled toward my shoulder.

"No! Please! Someone!" I jerked my head sideways, tearing clumps of hair loose in a burst of pain. It didn't help. The Thornwood dragged me toward its hungry branches, and there was nothing I could do to stop it. I couldn't even slow it down.

I braced both hands on the windowsill, trying to keep myself inside. Another branch shot over the stone and dug its thorns into my other wrist.

Then someone grabbed me from behind and pulled.

This did nothing except send new agony shooting through my arms, but at least I knew someone was trying to save me. *It must be Varian*, I thought. *He is a hero; I'll never doubt it again.* I let out a high-pitched sob, just as the person gave up on pulling me free and dashed beside me instead.

It was the kitchen boy.

My relief vanished instantly; *he* wasn't going to be able to save me. I drew in my breath for another scream just as the kitchen boy raised both arms over his head, and I saw that he was holding a sword. He brought it down on the windowsill, two inches from my fingers, and sliced the branches in half.

They hissed as if they had been burned. The boy raised the blade again, its point tilting and wobbling—the sword was clearly too heavy for him—and brought it down with less force this time. It barely dented the branch that was tangled in my hair.

The branch withdrew anyway, in one swift jerk, taking a chunk of hair and what felt like half my scalp with it.

I stumbled from the window. One heel hit something and I fell on my backside with a thump and continued scrabbling away. The kitchen boy followed, dragging the sword clumsily with him. It cut an ugly, uneven gash in the rug.

On the other side of the window, the Thornwood was dark, stirring occasionally as if because of wind.

A gnarled chunk was still attached to one of my wrists. I pulled it free, ignoring the pain as the thorns came out, and threw it at the window. It landed next to a tangle of dead branches, which was what I had tripped over. Several bright red spots of blood welled from my skin where the thorns had dug in.

"What just happened?" the kitchen boy gasped.

His hands were clenched around the hilt of a huge sword decorated with elaborate gold designs and set with a brilliant blue gem that must have been a sapphire.

"I don't know," I said. "What is *that?*"

"It's the prince's sword."

"What? The prince lost his sword in the Thornwood!"

"No, he didn't," the kitchen boy said. "He hid it here in the castle. Before he went into the princess's—your sister's—room, he stashed the sword behind a statue."

The branches wrapped themselves around my blade and wrested it from me, Varian had said. Why would he lie about that?

"I saw him do it," the kitchen boy said, "and after I left the kitchen, I decided I should have told you. I went to get the sword, and then came to get you—one of the chambermaids saw you headed down the servants' passage. When I heard you scream, I ran toward you, and . . . well . . ."

"You saved my life," I finished. "*Thank* you."

His face turned red. "It is, um, it is my honor to serve you, my lady. I mean, Your Highness."

"My name is Briony," I said. "What's yours?"

"Edwin."

"Well, Edwin, you have my . . . uh, my eternal gratitude." That didn't seem like enough. "Once we get out of the castle, I'll also give you lots of jewels and make you rich." Would my parents let me do that? And did we even *have* jewels? I knew from eavesdropping that the royal treasury was in trouble. It had been ever since my father had outlawed spinning wheels. We'd been importing all our yarn for sixteen years, and it didn't come cheap.

I squatted and peered carefully at the jewel in the sword hilt. Yup. Definitely a sapphire.

"Although," I said, "you could get rich just by selling this sword. You know that, don't you?"

"Sure," Edwin said. "Eventually. While we're in the castle, though, I thought it might come in handy for rescuing princesses."

I straightened and stared at him.

"Or," I said, "it might come in handy for getting us *out*

of this castle. If we have the sword, we can cut through the Thornwood!"

My voice went too high, and ended on a quaver. Edwin looked at me carefully. I tensed, waiting for him to say something stupid. Like *Don't be afraid.*

"We can't do it ourselves," he said. "This thing is so heavy I'm not sure I could swing it again. We need a trained swordsman."

"We're in a castle," I said. "It's full of trained swordsmen, all sworn to protect the king and queen. Once we find my parents and explain ..."

Edwin raised one eyebrow. It was the one that still had flour dusted on it. "Can we put the sword back in its hiding place first? It's a bit awkward to be dragging around. And I'd rather the prince not find out that a commoner took his sword."

The prince, apparently, had hidden the sword in a cobweb-covered nook half-hidden by a stone statue of a mermaid. Together, Edwin and I managed to lower the blade behind the statue. When we dropped it, it hit the end of the mermaid's tail with a clang that echoed through the hall. I winced.

"Don't worry," Edwin said. "If no one heard you screaming earlier, they're not going to hear *that.* The walls in this castle must be really thick."

I peered behind the mermaid to make sure the sword

was stable, then stepped back. The mermaid's nose was chipped, making her look like she was sneering at us.

Edwin cleared his throat. "You said you want to find your parents. But why don't we get the prince to cut through the Thornwood first?"

"The prince," I said, "told me that his sword got lost in the Thornwood."

"I think he was lying."

"Thank you. I got that on my own. But why would he lie?" I wrapped my arms around myself. "Maybe he wants us all to die in here so he can make off with our riches." Not that we had many riches . . .

"You're jumping to conclusions," Edwin said. "Maybe he was just being cautious. He probably wanted some time to make sure everything was safe before he let us out into the world. I mean, he had no idea who—or what—is really in here."

I thought of the fairy I had seen in the tower room. Maybe the prince had a point.

"And he's the one who cut his way through the Thornwood the first time, right?" Edwin went on. "He's the logical person to get us out."

I opened my mouth, then closed it. But my expression must have given me away, because Edwin's eyebrows slanted down. "Do you not like him?"

"He hid his sword behind a mermaid statue," I said.

"That doesn't exactly inspire confidence. For one thing, there are at least a dozen better hiding places in the castle."

Edwin burst into laughter, so loudly it made me jump. I'm usually the only one who thinks I'm funny.

"He's probably not in the habit of hiding things himself," Edwin said once he had calmed down. "Back home, I'm sure he has a servant whose sole job is to hide his extra candy and the books his parents don't approve of."

Now I was the one who laughed. "I guess you don't like him, either?"

"I wouldn't say that," Edwin replied hastily. "I've only gotten one glimpse of him. I just . . . you know. He's a prince. Royalty makes me uncomfortable."

"I'm a princess," I pointed out.

"A cake-throwing princess is a lot less intimidating than a sword-wielding prince."

"I'm not sure," I said, "if I should be insulted."

"I'm sorry," Edwin said quickly. "I didn't mean—"

"Don't worry," I said. "I'm used to being insulted. I can handle it."

Edwin's brow furrowed again. "How could anyone insult you? You're a *princess*. Don't people respect you?"

I stared at him for so long that he stepped back. "Beg pardon," he muttered. "Now what did I say?"

"Nobody in this castle," I said, "has *ever* respected me."

"Um." He bit his lip. "I'm sorry?"

"I'm not important enough to be respected. Everyone knows that." I narrowed my eyes at him. "Why don't *you* know that?"

"I ... um ..."

There was only one possible answer. "You're not from this castle," I said. "Are you?"

"Um ..."

"Stop saying *um* and answer me! Who are you, and why are you here?"

Edwin hunched his shoulders. "Remember that I just saved your life, okay? So you can't get too angry at me."

"Fine. Instead of making you rich, I'll reward you by not getting angry at you."

"I don't actually think it has to be *instead* of—"

"Edwin!"

"Right." He cleared his throat. "You're correct. I, um ... I don't actually work in this castle."

"Then what," I demanded, "are you doing here?"

Edwin lifted his chin. When he met my gaze, his eyes were pleading, but also defiant.

"I sneaked into the castle," he said. "I wanted to be here when your sister pricked her finger. I wanted . . ." He stopped and took a breath, then went on. "I wanted to sleep for a hundred years."

"Why?"

"Because in a hundred years," he said, "my master would be dead."

"I don't—"

"In the village, I was apprenticed to the blacksmith. He was . . . not a good man. He got angry a lot, and drunk, and he let the other apprentices—" Edwin winced. "It doesn't matter. He's dead by now. They all are. I'm free of them, just like I planned."

It took me a moment to find my voice. "But everyone

else you know is also dead! There must have been another way you could escape."

"There wasn't." He looked away. "You . . . you were never in the village, or you would have heard of me. The village dolt. That was one of the kinder names they called me."

I started, then tried to hide it. I *had* heard that name, that time when my governess had let me play with the village children. I vaguely remembered seeing a gawky figure on the edge of the town square.

Who's that? I'd asked one of my playmates.

The village dolt. He's not important. Throw me that ball!

And I had turned away. He had radiated a pathetic neediness that made me want to pretend not to see him.

Luckily, Edwin was still too sunk in memory to pay attention to my reaction now. "I came here to get away from everyone I knew," he said. "Every single person in the village despised me. I . . . I wasn't very good at being a blacksmith's apprentice. Or at playing games. Or at doing anything that mattered."

"Oh," I said, "I'm sure that's not . . ." He gave me a look, and I stopped. I had no idea whether it was true. "I mean, it's all right."

"Not really," Edwin said. "I was just a waste of space. The blacksmith didn't want to deal with me, but he couldn't make my parents take me back—they couldn't afford to feed me. So he just took on other apprentices, better ones, and they didn't think I should be getting a share of the food. They didn't really think I should exist at all."

"That's awful," I said fiercely.

Edwin raised his shoulders so high they nearly touched his ears. "They wanted me to just disappear," he said. "And I wanted it, too. That's why I came here."

"Well, I'm glad you did," I said. "And they were all obviously wrong about you. Look at what you've accomplished already. You're a hero."

Edwin snorted, but the corners of his lips quirked upward. "I think that's someone else's role. Someone taller and princelier."

"You've been here less than a day," I said, "and you've already rescued a princess with a magic sword. Sure, it was the *wrong* princess. But it's still a good start."

Edwin laughed.

"To be fair," he said, "you always struck me as quite competent, for a princess. So I suspect you're easier to rescue than your sister is."

I blinked. "Did we . . . Have we met before?"

Oh, no. Did he remember me from the village?

"Of course we have," Edwin said. "We met in the castle

this morning." He looked me over carefully. "You don't remember, do you?"

"I don't remember much from this morning." And I didn't know why. "So, um, we met already? How did that go?"

Edwin looked down. "It was so embarrassing, I don't want to speak of it."

My face went hot. Then I saw that he was fighting a smile, and I mock-punched him.

"You were very nice to me," he said, dodging. "I told you I was newly hired and lost. You showed me how to get to the kitchen. Then you stood there, looking around like you were waiting for someone, and when I asked, you said your friend Margot had promised to wear a dress that matched your sister's birthday cake and you wanted to see it."

I blushed again. Margot was one of the kitchen girls, and I had thought she was my friend. She was bubbly and round, with hair that sprang from her scalp in tight curls, and she liked to play a card game called Beanstalk. We used to play for hours.

But she'd lied when she told me about her dress. She had never planned to come to the castle on Rosalin's birthday. And she hadn't told me that.

Maybe she wanted to, but she was afraid I would tell

my father. Or maybe the other girls had pressured her out of it. . . .

Stupid, pointless hopes. Anyhow, I would never know now. Even if—*when*—we got out of the castle, what was I going to do? Ask her grandchildren if she had ever talked about me?

Edwin watched my face. His voice softened. "I knew Margot from the village. She mentioned you once. She said you were very kind."

I gave him a skeptical look.

"What? You do seem very kind."

I hoped I was. But Margot wasn't. I doubted she had ever spoken a word to the village dolt, about me or anything else.

"You're kind, too," I said, "for trying to make me feel better. But Margot isn't important anymore. The only people who matter now are the ones who are trapped in this castle with us."

Edwin snorted. "It seems to me there are only two people who matter: your sister and her prince. The rest of us are just sitting around waiting for the consequences of whatever they do."

My shoulders twitched. His words made me feel like something was itching at the inside of my skin.

"When I saw you the second time this morning," he added, "I was following your sister, because I wanted to make sure she would actually . . . you know. Prick her finger. Everything depended on whether she did. I saw you lead her to the tower—"

"You saw me do *what?*" Once again, I searched my memories. Still nothing after I left Rosalin's room. "Are you sure it was me who was with her?"

"She was saying that your hair looked like a bird started building a nest in it, then gave up halfway through."

"Definitely me, then." I chewed my lower lip. "And *I* was leading *her* into a room with a spinning wheel in it? Are you sure?"

"Definitely. I was paying close attention. You looked exactly the way you do right now—scared, but also brave and determined."

Was *that* how I looked? I tried not to ruin it by blushing yet again.

Brave. Determined. *And* I knew where the magic sword was. Combined, those three things led to one conclusion: there were more than two important people in this castle. Because Edwin and I were going to be the ones to get us out of here.

"Come on," I said, and whirled. My dramatic gesture was slightly ruined when I tripped over my hem, but I recovered and marched grandly toward the stairs.

I was somewhat relieved when Edwin followed me. I must have looked like I knew what I was doing, and even though I *didn't* know what I was doing, the fact that I could look like I did made me feel oddly confident. I slowed down so Edwin could walk beside me, and gave him what I hoped was a gracious and self-assured smile.

"Thank you for accompanying me," I said. "Once we are free, I will make certain that you are rewarded."

"That's great," Edwin said, "but do you actually know what you're doing?"

So much for that. "Of course I do."

"Do you know it well enough to explain it to me?"

"That . . . might be difficult," I admitted.

Edwin chuckled. For some reason, that made me feel even better than thinking he believed my charade.

"Come on," I said. "Let's keep going. It's time for us to find a way out of here. And we don't need a prince to do it."

9

We passed a pair of laundresses, then encountered a nobleman in the middle of the stairwell. Edwin faltered, but I strode forward without slowing down. The nobleman stepped aside at the last second and watched us pass with hard, angry eyes.

I wondered why the people still here had chosen to stay. Had they believed we would manage to escape the spell? Had they had nowhere else to go? Had they decided that staying in a castle, even a cursed one, was better than setting out into the world on their own?

I also wondered how long the castle could function without servants. They kept the place going. For example: Where would breakfast come from? My stomach was letting out embarrassingly loud rumbles.

So when we got to the royal sitting room, I was relieved to find my parents there. But I was even happier to a see a plate of pastries on one of the tables. They smelled like cinnamon and sugar and strawberry jam and had clearly been meant for Rosalin's party.

I was less excited that Varian was there, too, sitting on the couch across from my parents. It was just him—Rosalin, presumably, was still in her room primping. I didn't want to tell the prince that we had found his hidden sword. Maybe I could find a way to get him out of the room while I explained things to my mother and father.

"Briony!" my mother cried. "I'm so glad to see you."

My father rumbled in agreement and opened his mouth. My mother went on before he could speak. "I sent a maid to your room to make sure you were all right, but she hasn't returned yet. I was starting to worry."

The poor girl was probably wandering all over the castle looking for me. I opened my mouth, then closed it. My mother's solution would be to send another maid after the first one, which would only double the problem. I would have to track down the maid on my own.

First things first. I curtsied to my parents, then went into the room and picked a cinnamon roll off the tray. I bit into it, and crumbs sprayed from my mouth, some flying so far that Varian had to brush them off his knees.

"Really, Briony," my mother said.

"Sorry," I said, meaning it. But I was still more hungry than sorry, so I grabbed a blueberry muffin. I tried to chew it more slowly. "Edwin, do you want one?"

Edwin hovered in the doorway. I could tell by his face that he was as hungry as I was, but he didn't move. "I, um, I'm not sure I should."

"No," my mother said, "you certainly should not." As usual, it took her very little time to shift from concern for my well-being to irritation with something I had done. "Who are you, boy? I don't recognize you."

Edwin looked surprised. He had probably assumed that the queen wouldn't recognize any of the common servants in the castle. But my mother was a master at keeping track of details. Ever since a forgotten invitation had led to a fairy curse, she had become extremely well organized.

I took another muffin and marched it over to Edwin. "Here."

Edwin shifted his feet nervously and made no move to take it.

"I command you to eat it," I said. "Do you hear that, Your Majesties? He has no choice."

My father sighed. "Go ahead, boy."

"It's not that," Edwin said apologetically. "I just, um, I don't like blueberries."

There was a moment of silence. Then a muffin went flying past my ear. Edwin caught it.

"That one's plain," Varian said, lowering his hand. He had thrown the muffin with excellent aim. "Better?"

"Yes," Edwin said. "Thank you."

He bit into the muffin, and I turned back to the room.

"Excuse me," my mother said, shooting Varian a disapproving look. "As you might have noticed, we are in the midst of a terrible crisis." Her voice trembled a bit. "The spell has . . . Rosalin has . . ."

My father cleared his throat. "We need to discuss how to move forward." He took my mother's hand. "Briony, if you're hungry, go to the kitchen and have them make you something."

"There's no *them*," I said. "Haven't you noticed? The servants are mostly gone."

From the way my mother's mouth tightened, I could tell that she *had* noticed. But my father just waved his free hand impatiently. "We will bring in new servants once the Thornwood fades away."

I swallowed the last piece of my muffin a little too fast. It went down in a hard, solid lump. "'Fades away'? Is that what it's doing?"

"Of course," my father said. "Now that the spell has been broken, the magic sustaining the Thornwood has vanished, and it will wither and die." He patted the back of my mother's hand. My father was very good at reassuring people, even when he had no idea what to do. It was a very useful skill for a king. "This has been a terrible shock to all of us. I truly believed that we—that Rosalin was going to escape the curse." His voice faltered for a tiny second. Varian and Edwin probably didn't even notice, but I knew my father well. "You just need to be patient, Briony. I know that isn't always easy for you—"

I strode past my parents to the window and pulled the curtains aside. I had to really *pull*, because several thorns were latched into the fabric. When I finally yanked one side free, it revealed a branch curled sulkily over the windowsill, its thorns clinging to the wall.

The branch jabbed at me, and I stepped back hastily.

"I think," I said, "that this is the opposite of fading away."

My father stared at the thorns. A thin wheezing sound came from his mouth.

"The spell is gone," I said, "but the Thornwood is growing. And it's coming after us."

My mother let out a shrill scream. From the doorway, Edwin sighed.

"That's a good idea," he said. "Since we're all trapped in here, why not cause a panic?"

My father turned. His eyes were wide and a bit wild. "What do you mean, 'trapped in here'?"

"Uh . . ." Edwin opened his mouth, closed it, and sighed again.

"There's no need to panic," I said. "I have a plan."

My mother's and father's expressions did not change. Varian, for the first time, looked alarmed.

"Don't be afraid," he began.

I shook my head. "You really need to stop saying that."

"We must do something!" my mother said. She pressed her hands to her mouth. "We must— We have to— Oh, oh, oh. What are we to do?"

My father cleared his throat. "Don't panic, my dear."

I wished Varian weren't there. But I couldn't think of any way to make him leave. And there was no way I would convince my parents that whatever I had to say was too important for Rosalin's future husband to hear.

Oh, well. "I know how we can get through the Thornwood," I announced.

"There is someone who can help us," my father said at the same exact moment. He was already on his feet. "We must find the royal wizard."

"The royal wizard?" My mother's voice went high with hope. "He's here? He's in the castle?"

"Wait," I said. "Listen to—"

"He was in the castle when the spell hit," my father said, his eyes alight. "One of the chambermaids saw him. He'll know what to do."

I looked at Edwin, but he was nodding as if my father made perfect sense.

I guess to an outsider, it *did* make sense. I wished Rosalin were here, instead of waiting demurely in her room with her ladies. I could have exchanged wry glances with *her*.

The royal wizard was an extremely impressive man, if by "impressive" you meant tall. He was highly educated, having graduated from a snooty school that taught sports you could only play using magic. And he was very powerful, which meant he often spent days locked up in his workroom, emerging only to tell us that he had been battling wild magic and just barely managed to save the world from destruction. Then he would tell us that something we had been doing—like using my great-grandfather's invisibility cloak or taking visiting nobles to the unicorn grove—was upsetting the delicate balance of magic in the world and needed to be stopped immediately lest the universe collapse around us.

In my entire life, the only spells I'd seen him perform were the ones that had created fireworks on my and Rosalin's birthdays. And when Rosalin had asked if the fireworks for her twelfth birthday could be gold and silver instead of multicolored like they usually were, he'd said that one had to consider all the consequences before altering long-standing tradition. Then he'd told our parents that we were meddling with dangerous magic and putting the world in jeopardy, and we both had to skip dessert for a week.

To get even with him, Rosalin and I had stolen his hat—a classic magician's hat, long, pointed, and covered with blue stars—and painted it orange. He'd announced that the fairies had done it, as a warning that his spells were getting too powerful for their liking.

He had *also* been the one to tell my father that if we banished all spinning wheels from the kingdom, we could outwit the fairies and prevent the curse from taking effect.

"Wait," I said. "The royal wizard isn't—"

I might as well not have spoken. My parents were already halfway to the door. My mother turned and smiled at us brightly. She was still breathing rapidly, but her voice was steady.

"We will be back shortly," she said. "Have some pastries!"

Edwin pressed himself against the door to let them pass. As soon as they were gone, I turned to Varian.

You're jumping to conclusions, Edwin had said when I'd shared my suspicions about the prince. Well, I hoped Edwin was right, because Varian was now our only option.

"Okay," I said. "Here's my plan."

"Um," Varian said. "I think your parents are . . . are taking care of it? If there's a royal wizard . . ."

"Does *he* have a magic sword?" I said. "No. But we do."

"We do?" Varian looked at me warily. "There's another one?"

"Sure. There are two magic swords. They're very common in this part of the world."

Edwin coughed hard in my direction.

All right, fine. Maybe it wasn't a great idea to be sarcastic to the guy we were depending on to save us. "We found your sword, Prince Varian," I said. "We know you hid it."

Varian's face turned beet red.

"I don't care," I went on. "As long as you help us now, I don't care why you did it. The important thing is, you have a sword that can cut through the Thornwood, and you've succeeded in making your way through once. We need you to cut us *out* of the Thornwood."

"Just us?" Varian said.

"Of course not just us! We'll get everyone out. Or cut the Thornwood down and set the whole castle free." I leaned forward. "Once we're out, our subjects will help us."

"What subjects?" Varian said.

"You said there's a whole village right at the border."

Varian coughed. "Er. Once the Thornwood comes down, you'll no longer be a princess. You realize that, don't you?"

"What do you mean?"

"Well, you know. It's been a while. You don't exactly have a kingdom anymore."

He said it like it was obvious. And it was, now that I thought about it. The people of our kingdom couldn't have gone a hundred years without anyone to run things. New rulers must have stepped in while we slept. They probably wouldn't be willing to step *out* just because we had woken up.

"That's all right," I said after a moment. "You're a prince. So once you marry my sister, we'll all be part of a royal family."

Varian made a strangled sound.

"Oh, come on. You risked your life to save her. Let's not pretend you're *not* going to marry her."

Varian scraped a flake of pastry from the corner of his mouth. "I don't know anything about her."

"Didn't you spend the entire morning talking to her?"

"Yes." His eyes softened. "And she is a marvel. I never dreamed she would be so wonderful. But . . ."

"She *is* wonderful," I said sharply. "So why wouldn't you want to marry her?"

"Briony," Edwin said. "Maybe this isn't the best time—"

"No, I want an answer." No *way* was Varian going to wake Rosalin up just to break her heart. I would not let it happen. "Is that why you hid the sword? So you could cut your way out and *abandon* her?"

Edwin edged into the room. "Briony, that's not really fair."

I knew it wasn't. But Varian was looking wild-eyed and panicked, so I also knew I had caught him in a lie— even if I didn't know exactly what the lie was. All I could do was keep lobbing accusations to see what made him flinch. "Or did you not want us to look at the sword too closely and realize how valuable it is?"

Varian shook his head. His lips were white.

I tried to come up with another accusation. It was surprisingly difficult. Why *had* he hidden the sword? It had to have something to do with the Thornwood. If he could use it to cut us free—

I blinked.

"You *can't* use it," I said. "Can you?"

All the color drained from Varian's face.

"Briony?" Edwin said. "What are you—"

"You can't wield a sword," I said. "You don't know how. *That's* what you didn't want us to see."

Varian drew in his breath. I stepped toward him.

"Tell us the truth," I said. "Who are you?"

10

The silence in the sitting room was complete. Varian opened his mouth, then closed it. His jaw trembled and went taut.

"You're not a prince," I said.

He shook his head.

"What are you? A peasant?"

"Not exactly," he said. "I'm a ... a commoner. But where I'm from, rank is not considered important."

Though he had considered it important enough to lie about. "Let me guess," I said. "Commoners don't learn to use swords."

"No. We don't." He sighed. "I do know how to defend myself. But I've always preferred pistols."

"What are pistols?"

"They're ... complicated. And not relevant."

Right. I focused on what *was* relevant.

The curse will be broken only when a brave and noble prince wakes her with a kiss.

No wonder the Thornwood still surrounded us. The curse wasn't completely broken.

Which meant the new question was, why was it even a *little* bit broken?

"If you don't know how to use a sword," I said, "why did you think you could cut your way through a magical forest with one?"

"Ah," Varian said. "So, um, that's not exactly what happened."

"Do go on," I said.

He coughed. "I was outside the Thornwood, collecting fallen thorns—we sell them to tourists—and I heard a musical trill. When I looked up, a path had opened in the woods, and there was a fairy standing in its center. She was holding the sword, and she gestured to me to follow her."

"So you *did?*" Edwin said.

Varian glanced at him. "Like I said, I'm a commoner. I was collecting thorns on a cold morning, before sunrise, without any food in my belly. Then a fairy offered me a way into a magical castle. I didn't question it, okay? I just went."

Edwin nodded, and a look passed between the two of

them—like Edwin completely understood what Varian meant and they both knew I didn't.

I continued to focus on what was important. "So you got to the castle just by . . . walking? Down a path?"

"Right." Varian coughed. "I was *holding* the sword the whole time, though. And it was very heavy."

Before I could come up with an adequate response to that, Edwin said, "And when did you decide to pretend you were a prince?"

"The fairy led me through the castle to your sister's room. The princess was lying there on her bed, so beautiful. . . ." His eyes went soft, and his voice trailed off.

I cleared my throat loudly.

"Right. Um, I might have lost track of time while I was gazing at her. When I looked up, the fairy was gone. But I knew the story. I knew what I had to do." His cheeks colored slightly. "I kissed her, and she woke. She called me her prince, and I—I never quite got around to correcting her."

"That's one way of putting it," I said.

Edwin's brow furrowed. "It doesn't make sense. If no one has ever passed through the Thornwood before, why would the fairy godmother open a path for you?"

"Maybe because the hundred years were over," I said, "and it was time for the curse to be broken. My question is—"

"It's been more than a hundred years," Varian said.

Silence again.

"How *much* more?" Edwin demanded finally.

Varian coughed. "The Thornwood—and your castle—have been here for centuries."

Centuries.

I tried to swallow, but my throat was too dry. I didn't know why several hundred years seemed so much worse than one hundred. But it did.

Focus. Focus on what's important.

Varian was tapping his fingers nervously against his leg. "Um," he said. "Could you maybe . . . not tell your sister about this?"

"About the fact that you're not a prince and you didn't fight your way through the Thornwood to save her?"

He sighed. "All right. I guess you have to."

"No, no," I said. "I was just clarifying." I looked around the room. "We need a bandage to wrap around your hand."

"Why?" Varian said.

"To explain why you're not the one wielding the sword."

Varian blinked. "You're going to keep my secret?"

I nodded. *For now.*

"Why? I haven't gotten the impression you like me very much."

"I knew you were hiding something," I said. "Now that I know what it is, we're fine."

Which wasn't exactly true. He was still lying to my sister, and there was no way I was going to help him do that. But we had a more urgent task at hand, and we needed his help. We could figure out the rest once we were free.

"I know where they keep the bandages," I said. "Let's go."

———◆———

I kept an eye out for Twirtle as we walked. But there was no sign of him—or of any of the animals that normally inhabited the castle. No hunting dogs sniffing for scraps, no cats lazing about.

It was a bit of a relief—especially about the cats, who had always found Twirtle's protected status both unfair and ridiculous. But it was also puzzling. So when we passed one of the kennel boys lounging on a bench in a hallway, I stopped and said, "Do you know what happened to the dogs?"

The boy looked up. His face was streaked with dirt and tears, and his eyes were red. "What's that?"

He really should have risen to his feet before speaking to me. I glanced at Edwin and decided to let it go.

"Er—I'm sorry about what's happened to you. To all of us. I'm—*we're* trying to fix it, and I was wondering—"

He laughed rudely, revealing crooked teeth. "*You're* trying to fix it, are you?"

I kept my voice even. "Do you know where the dogs are?"

"Not in their kennel. That's empty." He grimaced. "The hounds knew what was coming. They were all desperate to get out that morning. Someone unlocked the kennel gate, and there was no stopping them. So I guess I'm out of a job." He looked past me at Edwin. "If you've come to the castle looking for work, you've chosen a bad day for it."

Edwin said nothing.

The kennel boy's eyes narrowed. "I recognize you. You're that useless boy from the blacksmith's shop. What business do you have in the castle, today of all days?"

Edwin remained silent.

The kennel boy shot to his feet, so fast I didn't realize what he was doing until his hand closed around Edwin's upper arm. "Answer me, sniveler. Why are you here? Are *you* the one who brought the spinning wheel into the castle?"

"Of course he's not!" I said. I was close enough to see how tightly the boy was holding Edwin. "Leave him alone."

"I don't need to hear from you, Princess," the kennel boy spat. "This is your fault, too."

Edwin's face went smooth and taut, like he could feel nothing. But I knew he was afraid and in pain. He was just very good at hiding it.

Because he was used to it.

A rush of fury went through me. I stepped forward. "Unhand him at once!"

The kennel boy looked me up and down and laughed.

I'm pretty used to being laughed at. Rosalin laughs at me an average of six times a day (I kept count for a while). But something about *this* laugh . . .

"Oho," the boy said. "The princess is commanding me, is she?"

I wanted to step back. Actually, I wanted to turn and run. And I'm pretty sure I would have, if not for Edwin's set face and grim, helplessly brave eyes.

Then Varian stepped up next to us. I hadn't noticed, until now, how tall he was.

"And you must be the prince," the kennel boy said. He tried to sneer, but his defiance wavered halfway through.

Varian waited, ominously silent.

The kennel boy let go of Edwin's arm. He stepped back and lifted his chin, but he wasn't nearly as good at hiding his fear as Edwin was. "Come to save the princess and forget the rest of us, have you?"

"We are going to save all of you," Varian said. His voice was quiet but somehow menacing. "And you are in our way."

The boy held his sneer for a fraction of a second. Then he turned and stomped down the hall.

"Well," I said after a moment. My voice shook, which was embarrassing—I wasn't even the one who had been attacked. But the sheer force of the kennel boy's hatred made me want to cry. I tried to copy Edwin's inscrutable expression. "He didn't have much courage, did he?"

"He was alone," Edwin said. "It's always easier when there's just one. It's impossible to get them to back off when they come in a group."

He said it matter-of-factly, like this was just a fact of life. Along the lines of *If you go outside when it rains, you'll get wet* or *It's not a good idea to insult fairies.*

I stood staring at him, until he noticed and flashed me an oddly apologetic grin. I looked away.

No wonder he had come here.

"In that case," Varian said grimly, "I suggest we avoid any *groups*. It seems there are some in this castle who blame the royal family for their plight."

"Then why did he go after Edwin?" I said, mystified. "It's obviously not his fault!"

Edwin massaged his upper arm. "Well, he couldn't exactly come after you, could he?"

My stomach clenched. I quickly walked on ahead so he wouldn't see my face.

Because the thing was, Edwin was wrong. He *could* come after me. Anyone could. I was princess of nothing; there was no kingdom around us, and I had seen zero members of the guard so far. There were very few people left in this castle, and it seemed most of them blamed my family for their predicament.

And their rage would grow the longer we were trapped here.

They *could* come after me. After me, and Rosalin, and our parents.

They could, and they would.

So we had to get out of here before they did.

———◆———

The palace apothecary was empty, which didn't surprise me. Our herbalist and our surgeon were a married pair, and they had children and grandchildren living in the village. They wouldn't have remained in the castle on the day of the curse.

The apothecary was also a mess. The pots on the shelves were knocked over sideways or smashed on the floor, and the dried herbs had been yanked from their hooks on the wall. The table was a mass of mixed herbs, smeared honey ointment, and shattered bits of clay.

I stood in the doorway, staring. The apothecary was my least favorite place in the castle—I had spent too many hours here having foul-smelling pastes applied to my hair. All the same, tears stung my eyes. Whoever had wrecked this place had done a savage job of it.

"Who could have done this?" I said.

Edwin's hand closed reassuringly around mine. "You saw how upset the kennel boy was. Angry people tend to break things."

"But—why the apothecary?"

"They probably came looking for something," Varian said. "Wine, maybe. And when they didn't find it . . ."

"Why wouldn't they find it?" I felt very stupid, like I was asking obvious questions. But I didn't know the answers.

"Because someone else found it first." Varian picked up a cracked jug, shook it upside down—nothing came out—and sniffed it. "Someone in this castle is very drunk right now."

"But the herbs are also all torn down," Edwin said. "What would anyone want from *them*? They're all just medicines, or . . . or . . ."

I swallowed. "Or poisons."

Edwin's grip on my hand tightened.

I pulled away and marched over to the cupboard where the bandages were kept. It was still closed, and its contents were intact. I pulled out a strip of white cloth. "Varian, hold out your hand."

He did. I blinked at it. "You're left-handed?"

"No," he said. "But since we're only pretending, I might as well have my right hand available for holding the sword. Just in case I need to."

"Don't you think Rosalin will have noticed that you're right-handed?"

"You didn't notice," Varian pointed out.

"Rosalin has been paying closer attention to you. She's half in love with you already, you know. She was before she ever met you."

Varian surprised me by flushing. "I know she's been waiting to meet me all her life. But until yesterday, I never imagined I would meet her. I didn't even completely believe she was real."

I started wrapping the bandage around his left hand, pulling a little tighter than was absolutely necessary. "What are you saying? That you don't like her?"

"No! She seems very nice. And she's extremely beautiful. I mean, obviously she's beautiful, that's the whole point of—ouch!"

I loosened up on the bandage. "You had better not hurt her."

"Why would I hurt her?"

Not a good enough answer. I stopped wrapping the bandage. "Swear to me that you won't, or I'll tell her the truth."

Whatever he saw on my face made Varian's eyes widen.

"I swear," he said. "I'll never deliberately hurt her."

I finished the bandage, tucked in the loose end, and examined my handiwork. It would not have been adequate if he had really been injured, but as a disguise, it would do. Medical techniques were *not* on the list of things Rosalin paid attention to.

"All right," I said. Ceramic crunched under my shoes as I headed to the door. "Let's go get that sword, and let's get my sister. And then let's cut our way out of here."

11

We found Rosalin in her room with four of her ladies, standing in front of her mirror in a voluminous gown. It was covered with so many white pearls that I couldn't tell what fabric the actual dress was made of. The ladies-in-waiting fluttered around her, making adjustments to her sleeves.

"Oh, Your Highness," one said. "You look so lovely." She was the lady I had seen earlier, the one who had been crying when she ran down the hall. Her face was wiped clean of tears now, and her voice was light, with only a slight tautness to her face to show how she was really feeling. "Your prince will fall in love with you all over again."

"He'll marry you in a heartbeat," said another. She knelt to examine the gown's hem, and I saw that her cheeks were streaked red, as if she, too, had scrubbed away tears. "And when he does, the Thornwood will dissolve and we will all be free."

So that was the story going around? Convenient. Though judging by the grim expression on the other two ladies' faces, I suspected that not everybody believed it.

Still, here they were, fussing with Rosalin's gown like it actually mattered what she wore.

I felt a tinge of scorn, but then I saw the first lady swallow hard and press the back of her hand to her mouth. Her expression reminded me of Edwin's as he struggled to hide his fear, and I was suddenly ashamed of myself. Of course they were doing what they were trained for, and telling themselves it might help. What else were they supposed to do?

"Rosalin," I said from the doorway. Edwin stood next to me, but Varian hung back with a nervous expression on his face, as if he was afraid I would change my mind and tell Rosalin the truth. (Which was smart of him. I wasn't sure I wouldn't.) "I need to talk to you."

Rosalin turned—carefully, because one of her ladies was arranging her hair. Varian was standing behind the open door, so she couldn't see him, but she flicked her gaze at Edwin. "Who's this?"

"This is Edwin. He's, um, a servant." I glanced at Edwin to see if he would take offense at that. He didn't seem to. He was staring at Rosalin with a slack-jawed amazement that was very familiar to me. It's the way everyone reacts when they get their first close-up look at my sister.

Mostly I don't mind, but sometimes it irritates me. This was one of those times.

Rosalin gave Edwin a dismissive look, then focused on me. "What's with your hair today? It looks like—like—"

"Like it was pulled out by magical thorn branches?" I suggested.

She blinked. "Well, yes. Exactly like that. Maybe one of my ladies can help you make it presentable."

Her ladies gave each other despairing looks.

Edwin looked at me, confused. "What's wrong with your hair?"

"Your ladies are busy," I said to my sister. "For starters, it will take them at least an hour to make that dress look less ridiculous."

Rosalin sniffed and ran her hands over her skirt. "I wouldn't expect you to know it, but this dress is the height of fashion."

"The height of fashion over a hundred years ago. Prince Varian will probably die laughing when he sees you."

Varian made a low, strangled sound.

"You look beautiful, Your Highness," one of the ladies-in-waiting said reassuringly. "Prince Varian will be enchanted. We just need to choose a necklace."

"Ooooh," I said. "I hope you have one with pearls."

Rosalin whirled. The motion shook several pearls loose, and they slid off her dress and rolled along the floor. One of her ladies scrambled to pick them up.

"Why don't you just leave?" Rosalin snapped. "Nobody needs you here. Go annoy someone else."

My chest went tight. "You *do* need me, actually. Even if you find that hard to believe."

She snorted, and two of the ladies-in-waiting tittered.

I clenched my fists. But really, what had I expected? Rosalin thought this was all about her, *her* fairy godmother and *her* dark curse and *her* dashing prince. I was just the insignificant little sister, who could never say or do anything important. Everyone thought so.

None of the stories mentions you.

But everyone was wrong. I was a princess just like her. I had even woken up before she had. And I was the one who was going to get us out of here.

The fairy's musical voice sounded in my memory: *Maybe today you're the important one.*

Something sharp and bitter and red-hot came bubbling out of me, searing my insides and spilling out of my mouth.

"You know what?" I said. "I wish the prince hadn't saved you. I wish you were *still* asleep!"

"Think for a second," Rosalin said cuttingly. "If *I* were asleep, you'd still be asleep, too."

"IT WOULD BE WORTH IT!"

She rolled her eyes. "Go fix your dress and fix your hair and fix your *attitude*, Briony. It's more important than ever that we act like princesses now."

"Sorry," I said. "I don't have enough pearls on me to scatter them around the room. If that's what acting like a princess means."

Behind me, someone laughed. I thought it was Edwin; but then, to my shock, I realized it was Varian.

Rosalin realized it, too. Her eyes went wide and her face went scarlet.

Varian stepped up beside me and bowed. "You look wonderful, Your Highness," he said. "Like a creature from my dreams."

Nope, her face hadn't been scarlet before. *Now* it was scarlet.

The ladies-in-waiting exchanged looks, then moved in sync toward the door. One of them pulled my hair, accidentally on purpose, as she walked past me into the hallway.

"However," Varian said, "your sister is right about the other matter. We must speak. If you have a moment . . ."

And for him, of course, she did.

There were a few problems with my plan.

First, none of us was strong enough to wield the sword. Edwin and Rosalin could both lift it over their heads and swing it down, but not for long, and they couldn't control it very well. I couldn't even get the point off the ground.

"Varian," I said.

He gave me a pleading look, but it had very little hope behind it. No matter how bad a swordsman he was, he was clearly the only one of us who had a chance of using the thing effectively.

"Why don't you try using mostly your right hand?" I suggested. "I'm sure it will be awkward and embarrassing, and obviously you won't be able to use it as masterfully as with your left hand." I gave him a meaningful look. "But at least you'll be able to swing it."

"It won't be embarrassing," Rosalin said firmly. She had fallen in with our plan surprisingly easily, probably because Varian had been the one to explain it. (And because we had fudged a few details, like how exactly the sword had reappeared. Luckily, it was hard to argue with "I don't know, it must have been magic!") "Varian is injured, and there is nothing shameful in that. But he will do the best he can, for our sakes."

Which was kind of true, so I couldn't even roll my eyes.

"I will be doing it," Varian said, his voice low and intense, "for *your* sake."

Oh, good. That definitely called for eye rolling.

But I found that I didn't quite mean it. The weight of what I knew sat in my gut, and I found it hard to look directly at my sister. The more she glowed at Varian, the more her eyes went soft and trusting, the worse I felt. Maybe being a commoner wasn't a big deal in Varian's day (not that I completely believed that), but it was a *very* big deal in our day.

I didn't know exactly how Rosalin would react when she found out the truth. But I was sure it wouldn't be pretty.

Oddly, the knowledge that I was wronging Rosalin didn't make me want to be nicer to her. Instead, it made me angrier at her. After all, if she hadn't been stupid enough to prick her finger on a spinning wheel, the Thornwood wouldn't be here in the first place.

And I wouldn't have this ugly, gnawing guilt in the pit of my stomach.

"Before we go," I said, "do you think you could change into something more appropriate for fighting magical trees with?"

"Good idea." Rosalin sniffed at me. "I see *you* were

smart enough to wear a dress that couldn't possibly look worse no matter what you did to it."

I looked down at my green dress with the dark stain near its hem. A memory of this morning—hundreds of years ago—swam up through my mind.

I left Rosalin's room, my chest hollow and aching. I reached my own room and called for my ladies-in-waiting. When they didn't show up, I got dressed myself, in the yellow silk gown I was supposed to wear for Rosalin's birthday. . . .

Panic climbed up my throat. "What happened to my yellow dress? This morning—I mean, that morning—I put on a yellow—"

"Mother made you change," Rosalin said. "Don't you remember? You weren't supposed to wear the yellow dress until the banquet."

I blinked at her.

"You threw an incredible tantrum about it. But honestly, Briony, it was a brand-new dress, and if you'd gotten it dirty before the banquet—"

"I don't remember," I said. "I barely remember anything from this morning. I mean, that morning."

Varian's brow furrowed. "How is that possible?"

"I don't remember anything, either," Rosalin said.

There was something odd about the way she said it—a lightness in her tone that didn't fit her words. Like she was relieved. But when she went on, her voice was somber. "I've been trying since I woke up. I don't remember *anything* from today."

No one doubted Rosalin, or told her to try harder. Varian made sympathetic, soothing noises and turned like he was going to hug her. Then he thought better of it—or maybe he felt my eyes burning holes into his back—and he squeezed her hand instead.

"You remembered my dress," I pointed out.

"That's the only thing."

"It seems like an odd detail to hold on to." Then again, maybe for Rosalin, it wasn't. I shrugged. "Though not as odd as the fact that we lost our memories to begin with."

"Well," Rosalin said, "we've all been asleep for hundreds of years, and there's a forest of thorns around the castle. So I think the standard for *odd* has moved a bit."

I grinned despite myself. "But it doesn't make sense. A lot of things don't make sense. Like, if you were the one who pricked your finger, why was *I* the one in the room with the spinning wheel? And how did you get out of that room and into your bed?"

"I guess . . . my fairy godmother moved me?" Rosalin winced. "You know. So the prince could find me. But why didn't she move *you*, too?"

"Because," Varian said, "it didn't matter where Briony was."

That was probably true . . . except there was something they didn't know: that I had woken before the spell broke. That the fairy godmother, after waking me, had asked me to spin for her. What if *that* was why she hadn't moved me? So I could spin?

Maybe today you're the important one.

A shiver ran up the back of my neck. I hadn't, after all, done what the fairy wanted. And she was still in the castle, somewhere. . . .

A flash of color in the corner of my eye. I whirled, my heart pounding. But it was only Edwin, holding up a section of Rosalin's delicate lace bed canopy and staring at it like he had never seen fine fabric before. When he saw me looking at him, he flushed and dropped it.

Rosalin went behind the screens to change, and I stepped closer to Varian. I spoke in a low voice. "As soon as we're free, you need to tell her the truth."

"Once we're free," he said, "it won't matter anymore."

"What does that—"

Rosalin stepped out from behind the screen, wearing a pink dress. It was as ridiculously covered with ruffles as the white dress had been with pearls, but at least the ruffles wouldn't go flying off the dress every time she moved.

"All right," she said. "I'm ready to be rescued."

She was speaking to Varian. But I was the one who led us out the door in the direction of the castle entrance.

12

In the corridor at the bottom of the stairs, we passed the royal treasurer, who was looking dour. That wasn't unusual. He had been under great stress my entire life, and met with my parents several times a year to beg them to revoke the spinning wheel ban. He said it was destroying the kingdom's economy.

As we rushed by him, Rosalin tripped and flew forward. Varian lunged for her, too late. Luckily, since she had changed her dress, no one got hit by any flying pearls. But the thud as her knees hit the rug made me wince.

Varian grabbed Rosalin's arm and pulled her to her feet. She shook him off and glared at the retreating treasurer. "You tripped me!"

The treasurer glared right back at her, then kept walking. He rounded a corner and disappeared.

Rosalin gasped. "How dare he!"

"It's all right," Varian said soothingly. "I'm sure it was an accident." He looked at me as if for confirmation.

I hadn't seen what happened, but I didn't really care. We had bigger problems than my sister's outraged dignity. "Yes," I said. "He should have apologized, but we'll tell Father, and he'll deal with it. Once we're out."

Rosalin sniffed and straightened her skirt. "Where was he coming from, anyhow? There's nothing down that hall but the kennels and the gardens."

Rosalin was right. What could the treasurer possibly have to say to the kennel master or the gardener? He considered himself high above their station.

Then again, he no longer had too many choices about who to talk to.

"Let's keep going," Varian said. "It doesn't really matter."

I wasn't quite as confident in our ability to figure out what mattered. But that wasn't why I remained where I was, looking down the hall and frowning. I was remembering the last time Twirtle had escaped, when we found him in the gardener's workshop, going through one of the seed packets. The gardener had *not* been happy, either about her missing seeds or about the bird poop on her floor.

"You know what?" I said. "Before we do this, we should go see the royal gardener."

"Why?" Varian said.

I had a feeling no one would be too thrilled about prioritizing a bird at a time like this. And they would be *right*, which would make it difficult to argue with them. So I said, "We're headed into a magical forest. A gardener might have some useful tips, don't you think?"

Varian looked skeptical. "Is she a magical gardener?"

"Not as far as I know." (Actually, I knew perfectly well she wasn't, but that would just lead to some more predictable and impossible-to-argue-with-because-they-were-true objections.) "I think we should talk to her."

"No," Rosalin said. "We know how to deal with the Thornwood. We have the sword. That's all we need."

"But—"

"*No*, Briony!" She strode ahead of us, her pink ruffles swishing against the rug.

"Well," Edwin said. "I'm glad someone's confident."

Varian hefted his sword and strode after Rosalin. Edwin and I exchanged a glance; then we shrugged simultaneously and followed them.

◆

As soon as we stepped into the castle entrance hall, I knew this wasn't going to be as simple as I'd thought.

And I hadn't really thought it was going to be that simple.

The hall was echoingly empty. There were no guards at the front gate, and none of the usual maids sweeping the floor. The front doors were open, but I couldn't see the courtyard through them. The doorway was covered by a wall of thorns, thick and solid, spikes and coiled branches forming an elaborate, grotesque design.

Other people had tried to get out before us. There were scraps of cloth caught in the brambles, and several of the thorns glistened wetly, covered with what I was pretty sure was blood. My heart stopped for a moment, but there was nothing yellow, and there were no feathers at all.

On the morning of Rosalin's birthday, I had opened the castle doors onto the courtyard, the ground slick and shiny with rain, shouts and neighs from the stables drifting through the warm air. The memory hit me suddenly, vivid but distant. Like something that had happened a very long time ago and gotten frozen in my mind.

———◆———

I was alone, finally. The last few days had been a chaos of fittings and cleaning, baking and decorating. Nothing mattered except Rosalin's party. The castle was all glitter and bustle and excitement, with a constant sour undercurrent of fear.

And Rosalin! She'd been avoiding me since morning, and the one time we'd met, she'd told me to try braiding my hair, which made me want to grab her hair, yank it out by the roots, and stuff it between her smug red lips. She acted as empty-headed as people assumed she was. As if this was just a grand party, attended by people coming from far and wide to admire her beauty. As if there were nothing to be afraid of.

Which left me to be afraid all by myself.

That was easier to do if I was actually by myself. And at last, I was. My ladies were busy with their clothes, my parents were busy with their preparations, and my sister had barely glanced at me since morning. It had been all too easy to slip away.

Good, I told myself. That's exactly what I want.

Normally the courtyard was a bustling place, especially on a brisk fall morning like this one. But today it was empty. I assumed that was because everyone was inside getting ready for Rosalin's party. A few colorful leaves floated past my shoulder, twirling and twisting as they fell. The air was cool and moist, disturbed only by the restless buzzing of insects. Above me, the foliage was an interlocking design of brilliant colors against a mostly gray sky.

An arc of blackness cut through the gray: a raven, soaring in a slow graceful spiral between leaves and sky. As I watched, the great black bird swooped low. It landed on one of the tower windows.

But there was something wrong. That bird was too big to be a raven. . . .

It cocked its head and looked straight at me, and then it wasn't a bird at all. It was a woman—a creature that looked like a woman—with shimmering dragonfly wings whirring behind her back.

She beckoned at me, and then she slipped through the window, into the tower, and disappeared.

———◆———

I gasped.

"Are you all right?" Edwin said. He was watching me closely, his eyebrows drawn together.

"I ..." I couldn't breathe.

"Briony?" Rosalin said worriedly.

"I'm fine." I would sort out the memory later. I didn't have time for it, not right now, not right here. The thorn branches weren't just outside the castle anymore. They filled the doorway, and several snaked along the inside wall, clinging to the edges of the thick tapestries. "Let's get started."

Varian picked up the sword and swung it awkwardly. Its point hit a vase and sent it flying. The vase shattered on the marble floor with a crash that made me jump, and a spray of flowers and colorful glass ricocheted across the entrance hall.

"Give me some room," Varian said.

We hastily complied. I backed up so far that my shoulder blades hit one of the tapestries. Edwin joined me a second later, his arm pressed against mine. Even Rosalin took several long strides back, though she kept her eyes fixed trustingly on her prince.

Varian glanced at her, and his face twisted with what I thought might be guilt. Or maybe I was just projecting my own feelings onto him.

"I'm not afraid," Rosalin assured him. "I trust you. Keep going."

"Rosalin," he said. "There's something I need to tell you."

"Not now," Rosalin said firmly. "There will be time for that later, once we're free."

Varian turned back to the door. He stepped forward and swung the sword at the thick, impenetrable mass of brambles.

It went through them like a knife through butter. Like they were *nothing*. The branches he cut through fell away, and then the branches below them crumbled.

The ground beneath was white cobblestone speckled with black, just like I remembered.

I gasped. "You did it!"

Varian looked over his shoulder and grinned. He stepped forward and swung the sword again.

When Edwin had used the sword, he had only managed to injure the branches and make them retreat. But in Varian's hand, the sword seemed barely to touch the thorns before they disintegrated.

Another step, and he was standing on the cobblestones. Outside the castle.

There was still a mass of sharp, tangled forest in front of him, branches arcing over his head and casting him in shadow. But the space behind him was clear, the ground bare, bumpy dirt and mud.

Edwin let out a relieved breath. "I have to admit," he said, "I didn't expect this to work."

"You didn't?" I said. "Then why didn't you say something?"

"I didn't think anyone would listen to me." He grinned. "I'm sure that's never stopped you."

There was something easy and unguarded in his tone. As if now that Varian was opening a path to the outside world, that strange future world where I wasn't a princess and there was little difference between kings and commoners, we were already on equal terms.

I found that I liked it. I returned Edwin's grin. "All right," I said. "Let's go tell my parents that we know how to fight the Thornwood. Then we can make a plan to get everyone out of—"

"No." Rosalin's voice sliced through mine. "We keep going."

Varian blinked. "But I thought—"

"Don't stop." She strode forward, stumbling as she did—Rosalin, who was so graceful she made walking look like dancing. "Cut a path straight through the woods, and we can walk out on the other side."

The sword dipped, and Varian strained to lift it. "But your father—"

"My father can't save me! He tried, and he failed. Nobody can help me, Varian." Her voice caught on a sob. "Nobody but you."

Varian's jaw tightened. He turned and swung again. The stroke was awkward and a little wobbly, but the thorn branches in front of him melted away.

"Do you really think," Edwin demanded, "he can keep this up long enough to cut all the way through?"

He had a good point. Varian's shoulders were already shaking.

But I didn't see how I could stop this. Nothing I said to Varian would mean anything, set against Rosalin's pleas or the tears now trickling down her cheeks.

So instead, I crossed the hall and grabbed Rosalin's hand. She shook her arm free and stepped closer to Varian.

This time, when he swung the sword, it shook so badly that even I could have knocked it out of his hands. But another chunk of the Thornwood gave way.

"Rosalin," I said. "Tell him to stop."

She put one foot on the cobblestones.

"Rosalin!"

"You don't understand." She stared straight ahead, her jaw quivering. "The fairy queen dwells in these woods. We've taken her by surprise, and that's the only reason we stand a chance. We have to cut our way out *now*."

"He won't be able to do it, Rosalin!"

"He can. He *can*."

"For you, I can do anything," Varian called. It would have sounded better if he hadn't choked on a breath while saying it.

He swung the sword again, more slowly. Sweat spotted the back of his shirt. Branches fell.

I looked at Edwin, then dashed forward and followed my sister.

Now we were past the cobblestones, and the ground beneath Varian's feet was dirt. The roots of the thorn trees coiled up from the dank earth; the trunks had grown winding around each other, forming an impenetrable wall. There was no way Varian could cut through that....

But he sliced the sword into one of the trunks. It bit deep and stuck, and then several trees crumpled as one, as if that shallow cut had been a fatal blow. A shower of dust and ashes fell to the forest floor.

Behind those stood more trees, thicker and darker. Branches curved over and around each other, gnarled and twisted and studded with sharp, wicked gray thorns.

Varian swung the sword again and the trees fell before him, and my heart leapt with hope. Maybe he could do it. He might not be a prince, but he was a hero. He was going to get us out.

"I don't think you have to swing so high," Edwin said, coming up beside me.

Varian wiped sweat out of his eyes, then swung again, lower this time. It clearly took less strength, and it worked just as well.

A hand closed around mine: Rosalin's.

"Come on," she said.

"Are we just going to leave *on our own*?" Edwin demanded. "What if the Thornwood closes up behind us?"

"We'll come back for the others," Rosalin said. "We'll cut our way through if we have to."

It sounded reasonable.

Edwin coughed skeptically. Shame washed over me. Why should *we* get to escape first? Were we really going to leave everyone behind, even temporarily?

"Why don't we go get them now?" I said. "Mother and Father can order all the men who are left to help with the cutting. They can take turns with the sword."

Rosalin's response was to pull me farther down the

path. Varian swung the sword again and slashed through another mess of thorns.

"Rosalin!" I dug my heels into the dirt and yanked my arm free. "Don't be so—"

Behind us, Edwin screamed.

13

The ground around Edwin exploded, clumps of dirt flying as barbed vines broke through the earth. One wrapped itself around his ankle. He reached down to yank it off, and another snapped around his wrist.

"Edwin!" I headed for him. A branch shot up in front of me, its thorns lengthening as it grew.

I tried to jump back but couldn't. A green vine had erupted from the earth and snaked around my shin. I pulled my leg frantically, but it wouldn't budge.

"Varian!" Rosalin screamed, and I turned to see that a thick thorny branch had wrapped around her waist. She grabbed it and tugged, then cried out and let go, blood dripping from her hands.

Varian swore and strode toward her, ripping the bandages off his left hand. Branches erupted around his feet, but none of them touched him. He pressed the edge of the sword carefully against the branch holding Rosalin, and it fell away from her in two dead pieces.

"Let's go!" he said, taking her hand. There was something new in his voice, a tremor I hadn't heard before. "Run, Rosalin!"

Rosalin pulled free. "No! Cut Briony loose!"

By now, the thorn branches were waist high and getting thicker. Varian swung his sword at a stand of them and came for me. A branch snaked around my other ankle.

Varian cut down one of the branches that had grabbed me—and a bit of my skin in the process, not that I was complaining. He turned and used the other edge of the blade to hack off the branch holding my other ankle.

Rosalin screamed again. A branch had managed to twine itself in her hair and was yanking her head backward. Meanwhile, Edwin had been pulled to the ground, and a thorny branch was crawling up his arm and over his shoulder.

"Help Edwin!" I shouted at Varian, and rushed to Rosalin, grabbing her hair and trying to pull it away from the thorns. She screamed bloody murder. I felt something bite into my ankle and dodged away from it, bringing a fistful of Rosalin's silky hair with me. She shrieked again: the thorns were still entwined in her hair.

"Hold her hair out straight!" Varian cried. "I'll cut it off!"

He had, of course, ignored my instructions and come for Rosalin. I looked past him. Edwin had been pulled down into a sobbing crouch; he was now nothing but a lump so covered with dark branches that in a few minutes, I wouldn't be able to see him at all.

I'm sorry, I thought. *I'm so sorry.* He had been right. We shouldn't have tried this on our own.

I looked up at the sky, the same way I had that morning hundreds of years ago. I could still see the tower rising high above the thorns.

And there, on the windowsill, a winged figure watched us.

"Fairy Godmother!" I shouted. "Help us!"

The figure didn't move.

"Briony!" Varian roared. "Hold out Rosalin's hair!"

I grabbed her hair and pulled it back. Varian's sword sliced right through it, leaving me holding a lank handful of limp strands with thorns still writhing through them. One thorn stabbed my palm, and I dropped the hair hastily.

Several vines erupted from the ground at once and pounced on the hair. Within seconds, they had sliced the black strands to shreds. As they shot upward, broken tendrils of my sister's locks fluttered from their thorns.

Rosalin clutched my hand. Her face was twisted with pain and terror. "Run!"

I tried. But a branch shot across my legs, and I tripped and fell. The second my hand hit the ground, another branch erupted between my fingers.

"Varian!" Rosalin cried. "Cut her loose!"

No. Help Edwin first. I tried to say it, but the words wouldn't come. Terror closed my throat. Edwin wasn't moving now. Branches climbed over him, growing from his hunched-over body. That would be me, in just minutes, if we didn't get out.

Varian sawed through the branch holding my hand down, and then through the vines around my ankle, and then he whirled and sliced off a branch that was reaching for Rosalin's neck. Together, the three of us staggered toward the castle doors. A branch struck at my ankle, and I savagely kicked it away. Varian stopped using his sword like a knife and instead swung it wildly in front of him. The blade cut through a swath of trees, which fell away like dust, clearing a space before us. For the first time, I believed we were going to make it back.

But not all of us. We had already passed the thorns growing over Edwin.

I forced myself to stop, even as the thorns bent toward me and every muscle in my body screamed *Run run RUN!*

I looked up. The black figure was still watching us, her dragonfly wings spread wide.

"Fairy Godmother!" I screamed. "Help us and I'll spin for you!"

The fairy didn't move. I sobbed, turned away from Edwin, and lurched forward, but I had stopped for too long. A branch was wrapped around my ankle. I reached down and yanked it. Pain pierced my palm and blood dotted the thorns, but the branch didn't move.

I looked up. A solid wall of trees had shot up before me, already so thick they blocked Rosalin and Varian from view.

Someone seized me by the shoulders, and a musical voice said, "Hush! Stop calling for fairies, you stupid child. I'm not the only one who might answer." The fairy pointed at the branch holding me down. "Cease to grow!" she commanded.

The branch dissolved, and the fairy lifted me into the air, her hands beneath my arms.

I screamed, and she snarled, "I said be quiet! My power is limited in my queen's woods. I'm doing what I can."

She shot upward so fast that the air was ripped out of my throat, giving me no choice but to obey.

The thorns writhed up toward us, but in less than a second, we were out of their reach. Before I had time to think about falling, the fairy deposited me on the sill of the tower window.

"All of us," I gasped. "I said *us*. My sister and her prince, and Edwin, too."

The fairy godmother hovered in front of me, her wings a blur. "You will spin extra for each human I save."

"Yes, yes. Just *get* them!"

She smiled her too-wide smile and dove into the woods, leaving me alone on the windowsill.

Below me, the tower stretched down, down, down into the branches. The tops of the trees thrashed in the wind, too far below for me to make out individual thorns.

All at once, I could think about nothing but falling.

The fairy had left me on the very edge of the windowsill. To get myself inside the tower, I would have to move sideways along the ledge until I reached the window. Stabs of fear crawled up from my feet and quivered through my body. One wrong move, one careless shift of weight, and I would fall screaming into those waiting thorns.

Dizziness washed over me, and the world tilted. I closed my eyes and clung to the cold stone with all my might.

A whoosh of air. I opened my eyes just in time to see

the fairy godmother deposit Rosalin on the windowsill next to me.

"Excuse me," I said. My voice shook. "If you don't mind, could you—"

The fairy whizzed downward and disappeared into the Thornwood.

Rosalin made a strangled sound. She got to her feet, inched along the narrow sill, and swung herself through the window. I heard a thump as her feet hit the floor.

"Briony?" she said. "Come on."

She made it look so easy. I leaned in toward her, and my hand almost slid off the smooth stone. I froze.

"Briony?" Rosalin's head popped through the window. Her face was marred by three long, bloody scratches and surrounded by a ragged mass of shorn tangles, but she still looked beautiful. That's fairy magic for you. "What's wrong?"

"I can't move," I whispered.

Rosalin frowned. "All right. Don't look down."

I looked down anyway. The thorns were a tangled blackness far, far below. There was no movement in the branches.

"I said *don't*, you idiot!" Rosalin said. "Look at me."

I looked at her. Rosalin had pulled herself halfway onto the sill and was leaning precariously over thin air so she could hold out her hand.

"Come on," she said soothingly. "Just move a little bit forward and I can pull you in."

Or I could pull her down. I looked over the side again.

"Stop doing that!" Rosalin said.

The Thornwood was back to the solid mass it had been before we started cutting through it. Shouldn't the fairy be back by now? Was it taking her this long to get Edwin free?

Was Edwin still alive?

I remembered the branches growing over his face, cutting off his screams. My gut wrenched, but at least I wasn't thinking about falling. I used that moment to slide one hand forward.

"Good," Rosalin said. "Now your leg—your right leg, so you stay balanced."

It sounded like a good idea, but my leg felt like it was made of stone—quivering, heavy, rubbery stone. I couldn't move it.

Rosalin slid farther out onto the sill. My stomach lurched just watching her, but she leaned right next to the edge as if it were nothing and took my fingers in hers.

"Don't pull me!" I screamed.

"I won't. Come on, Briony. You can do it. Don't be afraid."

"Did you ever notice," I said through gritted teeth, "that people only say 'Don't be afraid' when there is a *very good reason* to be afraid?" But as I spoke, I managed to slide my leg forward, scraping my knee over the stone.

"Good," Rosalin said. "Now your other hand. Just like that."

I obeyed. Once I had started, it wasn't hard to keep going. All I had to do was focus on the movements, and not think about the drop just inches away. Not think about how if I slipped, I would plummet like a rock. . . .

"Don't stop!" Rosalin said.

I pulled my left leg forward, then my right hand. Then my right leg, and my knee caught on a bump in the stone, and I tilted sideways and screamed.

"You're fine." Rosalin's hand tightened on mine. "You're *fine*."

But I could hear the panic in her voice. That had been close.

Stupid fairy godmother. Why hadn't she just put me through the window?

Hand. Foot. Hand. Foot.

Then Rosalin grabbed me by the shoulders and pulled me inside, and we tumbled together onto the cold stone floor in the shadow of the spinning wheel.

14

We lay on the floor clinging to each other. Rosalin wrapped her arms around me, and I buried my face in her shoulder while trying to figure out whether I was going to cry.

It took me a moment to realize that *Rosalin* was crying.

"I got separated from Varian," she gasped. "The trees came up between us, and he—he kept going, Briony. He didn't come back for me."

I sat up. Much as I didn't like Varian, I knew what I had heard in his voice when he was begging her to run. He had been terrified for her. "That can't be true, Rosalin. He must have tried—"

"But he *couldn't*, Briony. All this time I've been waiting for someone to save me, and now my prince is here and there's *still* no one who can help me."

My prince. I winced. But this wasn't the time to tell her

the truth. I leaned forward, meeting her eyes through the ragged veil of her hair. "That's not true. *I* helped you."

She wiped tears from her face.

"Well," I amended, "I got your fairy godmother to help you."

There was a thump at the window, and we scrambled to our feet.

The fairy godmother crouched on the sill. A bruised and bloody creature dangled from her hands: Edwin. He was unconscious, his clothes in shreds and stuck to his body with dried blood.

I gasped. "Edwin!"

"Where's Varian?" Rosalin demanded at the same time.

The fairy tossed Edwin into the room. He landed hard on the stone floor and flopped onto his side. I scrambled over to see if he was breathing. He was, but the breaths seemed shallow. Was that normal for unconscious people? I had no idea.

"Your prince is safe," Rosalin's fairy godmother said to her. "He cut his way back into the castle."

Rosalin let out a breath. "You're sure?"

"Oh, yes. It was easy for him, once he was freed from the burden of protecting you."

Rosalin pressed her lips together. Her cheeks were still stained with tears, but when she spoke, there was no hint of the doubt she had expressed to me. "Is that meant to be an insult? He *came* here to protect me."

The fairy godmother spread her wings. The sunlight slanted through them, casting a shifting pattern on the floor. "Did you happen to notice, when you weren't screaming, that none of the thorn branches reached for *him?*"

"Because he had the sword!" Rosalin said.

"Are you sure?" The fairy's eyes gleamed yellow. "How certain are you, Princess Rosalin, that you truly know who your prince is?"

"What about Edwin?" I demanded.

The fairy cast him a quick glance. "Oh, *he's* who he says he is."

"I mean, is he safe? Is he going to recover?"

She shrugged. "I'm not sure."

"Can you help him?"

"I could." She tilted her head. "What will you give me in return?"

"I said I'd spin if you help us. He's part of 'us.'"

"Since when?" the fairy snorted. But she leaned over and gathered up Edwin's body, moving with an easy, delicate grace. Her dragonfly wings shimmered with constantly moving color, like sunlight seen through lowered eyelashes.

"I'll be back shortly," she said, and vanished.

A moment later, the door slammed open, and Varian staggered into the room. He looked around frantically, then focused on my sister.

"Rosalin!" he gasped. "You're all right?"

"I'm fine, too," I said. "Thank you for asking."

Varian and Rosalin ignored me. They stared at each other for a few intense seconds. Varian stepped toward Rosalin and reached for her hand, and Rosalin tilted her chin up. I was too worried about Edwin to care about the kissing that was clearly coming, but I averted my eyes anyhow.

Then Rosalin said, "Who are you?"

I looked back swiftly. My sister's eyes were cold, and her voice was hard.

Varian blinked. He was so taken by surprise that he continued to bend over her, and his lips were only inches from hers when he caught himself and jerked back. "What?"

"My fairy godmother told me you weren't who I thought you were," Rosalin said. "What did she mean by that?"

"Nothing!" I said quickly. "She's probably just trying to confuse us. Don't let her do it."

Rosalin gave me a version of the same icy look she was giving Varian. I had seen it a hundred times, so it didn't have the same effect on me. I glared back.

"Don't get distracted," I said. "Varian is on our side, and I'm not sure that's true of your fairy godmother. We need to work together."

"And in order to do that," Varian said, "we need to be honest with each other."

No, I thought at him as hard as I could. *No, we don't.*

"I can't lie to you," Varian said to Rosalin. "Not anymore."

Yes, you can. Just try!

"I want you to know . . ." He faltered. He reached for my sister, then let his hand drop. "I . . . I need to explain something to you."

A shadow of fear passed over Rosalin's face. But she stepped closer to Varian and took his hand in hers.

"Come," she said softly. "Let's go someplace where we can talk."

And without a backward glance, they walked out the door and down the stairs.

———————◆———————

I was pretty sure they expected me to follow them. Instead, I looked at the spot where Edwin had fallen, remembering his bruised face and the blood stuck to his clothes. The fairy godmother had said . . . or at least implied . . . or, well, it was *possible* that she was going to bring Edwin back here once she had cured him. Or whatever she was doing. I couldn't leave until I saw with my own eyes that he was all right.

But also: I didn't really want to be anywhere near Rosalin right now. When Varian told her the truth, he would also tell her that *I* had known the truth.

She would forgive him, sure. He was her true love, her hero, the reason she wasn't sleeping for another thousand years. She had to forgive him.

She didn't have to forgive me.

She hadn't even come after me yet, and already my shoulders were knotted. I tried to shore up my defenses, to get angry at her before she could get angry at me. Why *should* I have told her? It wasn't like she ever listened to me.

It didn't work. Guilt kept creeping back in. I didn't even like Varian, yet I had chosen him over my own sister. I had helped him deceive her, and now she was going to get her heart broken and it was my fault. I couldn't even remember why I had done it.

No, that wasn't true. I knew exactly why I had done it: Because I was scared. Because all I had been able to think about was getting out of the castle.

That was also why I had led everyone out into the Thornwood. Edwin was the one who had paid for that. He'd come here to get away from people who had hurt him, and now, thanks to me, he was hurt more than he ever would have been in the village.

When the fairy godmother appeared, it was a relief.

At least, it was until I realized that she was alone. I clenched my fists. "Where's Edwin?"

"He's all right," the fairy godmother said. "I healed him and left him to sleep it off."

"Left him where?"

The fairy godmother looked amused. "Concerned about him, are you? What a fondness your family has for commoners." She pursed her lips. "But as I recall, you used to chase after the kitchen maids the same way."

I flushed. "Edwin has fought the Thornwood with me. *Twice.*"

"I'm not denying it." She shrugged. "My spell worked out quite well for you, didn't it? Most of the people who know how useless you are died long ago. You have a chance to start over with new people who haven't realized it yet."

She didn't emphasize the *yet*, but it seemed to echo in the round stone room.

"Unless," she went on, her lips curving unnaturally high and cutting into her cheeks, "you turn out to be quite important after all. Unless you turn out to be the key to the survival of every single person in the castle."

She spread her wings and rose several inches into the air. "Spin for me."

It still didn't seem like a good idea. But I had promised.

Besides, we had just tried, and failed, to cut our way out of the Thornwood. The magic sword wasn't going to be enough. We needed more powerful magic.

We needed *fairy* magic.

The fairy godmother was our only hope. And since I was the one she seemed interested in bargaining with, I was the castle's only hope. Just as she had said.

"I won't tell you where the boy is," the fairy godmother said, "until you spin." She swept her wings back and forth, waiting.

"But why do you want me to spin?" I said. "What do you gain from it?"

Her eyes glittered. "The thread from this spinning wheel has great power. It can trap the fairy queen herself, if you wield it right."

"Then why don't you spin some yourself?"

"The magic requires human energy. You will spin some of your life force into the thread, and that is where its power will come from."

I crossed my arms over my chest. "If I'm going to give you my life force, I think you owe us more."

"Barely a trickle." She waved a hand through the air.

"You humans have such an abundance of life, and you have no idea how to use it. There is so much we can do with the minutes you fritter away playing games, the breath you waste on chatter, or just a few drops of your blood."

Her voice dipped hypnotically low, the magic in it so compelling that it almost didn't matter what she was saying.

"Um," I said a bit desperately, "using a spinning wheel is probably *hard*. I can't just start spinning thread without any instruction or practice or—"

She smiled, her lips stretching from one side of her face to the other. "Give it a try."

Still I hesitated, and she dropped to the floor. Her feet didn't make a sound when she landed. "Come, Princess. Start spinning and I'll answer your questions. I promise."

"Why can't you just answer them now?" I demanded.

The fairy licked her lips. Her tongue was too long; when she flicked it, it reached all the way to the end of her chin. "There are rules, Princess; fairy laws that run deeper than blood. We cannot do as we will, especially not in the human world. Our queen laid down the laws eons ago, and all fairies are bound to them. When we deal with humans, there is always a price, a bargain, an exchange."

There was a firmness to her words that made her impossible to doubt. I took a step toward the spinning wheel before realizing what I was doing.

"How would I even know," I said, "if you're telling the truth?"

"Fairies always keep their bargains. You must know that."

Everyone knew that. I was just stalling.

I walked up to the spinning wheel. The fairy godmother's wings fluttered, sending rainbow reflections scattering across the walls. I settled on the stool and put both feet on the pedals that would make the wheel spin.

"I need wool to feed in," I said.

"No." The fairy godmother's eyes were bright, like there was a dark light leaking out of her pupils. "You don't."

I closed my fingers in midair, as if around a tuft of wool. I imagined I felt it sliding through my fingers, soft and scratchy against my palm. I opened my eyes and it was there, dingy black wool appearing in my hand out of nowhere.

I gave the wheel a slight push with my other hand and began to spin.

Gold thread spun out of the smooth wood and wrapped around the bobbin. My legs were too short for the pedals, so I had to tilt the stool forward, but even with that, the movement felt easy and natural. As if I had done it before.

Had I done this before?

How did I know that the pedals made the wheel spin? That I had to pull the wool out as I fed it in, give it enough twist to make sure it didn't break, and use one hand to pull on the fibers while holding the front threads steady with the other? I had never seen a spinning wheel; they had been illegal my entire life. Yet my legs moved smoothly, making the wheel whir steadily, and my hands fed in black wool, and the wheel pulled it through and twisted it into golden thread.

I drew too fast, and the thread went thin and broke. I grabbed it swiftly with my right hand, smushed it with the wool in my left hand, and kept going without slowing my pedaling.

I was good at this.

I was very, very good at this.

And I shouldn't even have known how to start.

I searched my memory for where this ability came from. Had I smuggled a spinning wheel—*this* spinning wheel—into the castle? Spun in secret? Could I really have been so selfish, so *stupid*?

I couldn't remember anything like that. I could have sworn that the first time I had ever seen a spinning wheel was when I'd woken from the spell.

But this clearly wasn't the first time I had used one.

The wheel made a whirring sound, with occasional faint clicks. The bobbin spun hypnotically, reacting to the rhythm of my feet. The spindle jutted out, sharp and thin, but it didn't seem to be doing anything to the wool—it was as if the only reason it was there was so people could prick themselves on it. Which struck me as a serious design flaw.

Or maybe that *was* the only reason it was there.

I stopped. The wheel whirred slower. The thread shone on the bobbin, a thick layer of silken gold.

I felt like I might throw up.

"Tell me now," I said. "How do I make the Thornwood go away?"

The fairy godmother turned her head so sharply that her hair whipped across her wings. "I must go. So I will trust you to keep your part of the bargain. You will continue spinning until the bobbin is full."

"Yes," I promised. "I will."

"Very well. The human who can make the Thornwood stop is your sister." She snapped her wings together and vanished. Dust motes swirled in the air where she had been, and her clear, musical voice echoed through the room. "And the way she can stop it is by dying in it."

15

The spinning wheel was still turning slightly when Rosalin and Varian walked back into the room.

They weren't arm in arm anymore. Varian's face was drawn, and Rosalin's was pinched. My stomach flipped when she looked at me.

"He's not a prince," she said in a hard voice. "And he's not a hero. He didn't fight his way through the Thornwood to save us. My fairy godmother *invited* him in." Rosalin kicked at a small stool near the wall, as if it was in her way. It fell over with a crash. "Apparently, he didn't think it was important to mention that small detail before risking our lives by taking us into the Thornwood."

"I know this is a shock," Varian said a bit desperately. "Even to you, Briony. I could tell you suspected me of something, but I'm sure it was nothing like this."

I blinked at him, and he gave me a small, firm nod. It was a moment before I understood.

He hadn't told her. He hadn't told Rosalin that I already knew, that I had lied to her. He was keeping my secret, just like I had kept his.

"I'm sorry I lied. To *both* of you," Varian went on. "I didn't know you. I only knew your story, or at least the version of it they told where I'm from. I thought I had to fit myself into that story in order to gain your trust."

"Um," I said. There was no way to thank him, not with Rosalin there. "That's all right. I understand."

He turned to Rosalin. "Does it really matter to you that I don't have royal blood?"

"That's not what's important," Rosalin said. "What matters is that you lied to me."

It was such an obvious answer. She almost had to say it.

But I knew it wasn't true.

Don't be convinced to marry below your station, Rosalin had told me once. We had been hiding from our language tutor, who was making us read a long, unlikely story about a princess who married a frog. (Or something. Since it was in Gnomish, it was a little hard to follow.) We both knew the story had been chosen to convince Rosalin to accept a marriage proposal from the duke's sixth son. *Don't let them think so little of you. This whole idea is insulting. I may be cursed, but I am still a princess!*

Varian's birth *did* matter to Rosalin. It would matter to anyone in this castle.

But Varian, who had come to us from a time when different things mattered, couldn't see what would be so clear to anyone else here. And so he believed her. He looked stricken. "I wanted to tell you."

Rosalin looked haughtily away, and Varian's face crumpled.

I drew in a breath. My sister's romantic complications were not enough to distract me from what I had just learned. The fairy godmother's words ricocheted back and forth in my mind.

Dying in it. Dying in it. Dying in it.

No, I thought.

"Briony?" Rosalin said suddenly and sharply. "What do you think you're doing? Get away from that spinning wheel!"

I opened my mouth, then closed it.

Dying in it. Dying in it.

I couldn't tell them. Especially not Rosalin.

The way she can stop it, the fairy godmother had said. Not *the only way to stop it.* So maybe there was another way.

"Briony!" Rosalin said. "Didn't you hear me? Get away from that thing!"

Varian raised his eyebrows and strode to the spinning wheel. He pressed a finger to the point of the spindle.

"Seems safe enough," he said, and grinned at me.

We both stared at him as if he had pulled his pants

down and started dancing a jig in his undergarments. His grin faded.

"It's not funny!" Rosalin snapped. "Do you think what happened to me is *funny?*"

"No! I was just making a— I didn't think— I shouldn't have—" He stammered to a stop. He looked like he was regretting not just what he had done, but having been born in the first place. "I'm *sorry.*"

"It's understandable," I said quickly. (Even though I didn't really think so.) "I guess spinning wheels aren't scary anymore. People must use them all the time."

"Well, no," Varian said. "We have better machines for making thread now. But in the village, they have model spinning wheels as part of their historical display."

Out of the corner of my eye, I saw Rosalin flinch. "Don't tell me," she said tightly. "They have festivals where people prick their fingers on fake spinning wheels for fun."

"Oh, no," Varian said. "Not at festivals. It's a common children's game. It's called prick-a-princess —"

"*Anyhow,*" I said. Varian stepped away from the wheel as if driven by the force of my glare. "I told the fairy godmother I would keep spinning gold thread for her, and now I have to do it."

"Gold thread?" Rosalin repeated. "Isn't that from a

different story? The one the minstrel always sings at dances?"

"Fairies always spin gold thread," Varian said. "They wouldn't bother spinning anything else. In every story I've heard, that is." He looked at me. "But do you really think spinning for her is a good idea?"

"I promised," I said. "Do you know what happens to people who break promises to fairies?"

"Um . . ."

"Okay," I admitted, "neither do I. But I'm pretty sure it's not good." I positioned my feet on the pedals. "Besides, the fairy godmother is the only one who can get us out of here."

By dying in it.

No. There had to be another way. I would bargain with the fairy until she told me, and then I'd bargain until she helped us. Even if I had nothing to bargain with.

"What makes you think she can help us?" Rosalin asked. "I heard her, when she was carrying you away. She said she doesn't have much power in the Thornwood."

"That makes sense," Varian said. Rosalin shot him a glare, and he hesitated, then went on. "The Thornwood belongs to the fairy queen, and your godmother is just an ordinary fairy. She can't go against her queen. I don't think it's possible for them."

"Look," I said as calmly as I could (which wasn't very). "She saved Rosalin from dying, and she saved us from the Thornwood, so she's on our side. Ish. She might know a way we can ..."

The way she can stop it is by dying in it.

My throat closed, and I knew I was about to cry.

But I couldn't. If I cried, they would want to know why, and I couldn't tell them. Once Rosalin got past being terrified, she tended to get all noble and stupid; she might very well decide to sacrifice herself to save the rest of us. Which was probably something most people wouldn't have thought her capable of, but everyone underestimated my sister.

"Get off that wheel," Rosalin said. "I forbid you to spin."

That got me to focus. "You *forbid* me?"

"Yes. You're being foolish."

I dug my fingernails into my palms. "You don't get to order me around. And I'm a lot smarter than you are. Maybe if you would just listen to what I said instead of acting like this is all about you—"

"It *is* all about me!" Rosalin said. "Do you think that makes me happy? Do you really wish this was about *you*, that you were the one cursed—"

"Are you really so sure that it's *not* about me?" I demanded. "I'm the one who woke up first! I'm the one your fairy godmother asked to spin! And I'm the only one who can see past the end of her own nose!"

Rosalin started toward me. I slid quickly back to the edge of the stool, and as I did, I caught a glimpse of Varian's expression. His lips were curved in amusement, like he thought this was funny.

"And if *I* don't spin," I finished, "I'm the one who pays the price! Don't be so—"

Rosalin made a whimpering sound. I looked at her, at her wide dark eyes, and the words I was about to say died on my lips.

Don't be so selfish. But that wasn't selfishness on her face. It was fear.

By dying in it. Did Rosalin know?

"Rosalin." I slipped off the stool. "Are you . . . are you afraid of your fairy godmother?"

Rosalin shook her head. Her hands were clenched so tightly her knuckles were white.

"Not of her," she said. "Of the other one. The fairy queen. The one who cursed me to die." She drew in her breath. "The one who's waking now."

Silence.

Rosalin forced her hands to her sides. "At my christening, my fairy godmother said that instead of dying, I would sleep for a hundred years. *And so would the fairy queen*. The minstrels forget that line, but it's the part that truly protects me. While I was asleep, the fairy queen would also sleep, and I would be safe from her."

Her eyes were wide with fear. It was exactly the way she had looked when she'd first woken up and seen me.

"That's why," I breathed. "That's why you were afraid when you woke up."

"I didn't realize I was awake at first," Rosalin said. "I thought I was still dreaming. The whole time I was asleep, I dreamed of princes. Hundreds of them. They had nothing in common, except they were all so hand-some . . ."

Her voice trailed off. Normally, I would have rolled my eyes, but now I just watched her.

". . . and they all kissed me. Every time, I thought I was about to wake up. I opened my eyes, *trying* to wake up, just in time to see the prince dissolve and disappear. And then I knew I was still asleep, and still safe from the fairy queen."

"Rosalin," I said. My heart hurt.

She shook her head. "I couldn't believe it was over. I *didn't* believe it. When I opened my eyes and he was still there, I thought it was just another trick." She drew in a deep, shaky breath. "Until I turned my head. And then I saw . . ."

"Me," I whispered.

"You. You were standing there with your arms crossed over your chest and your hair looking like a goblin's half-eaten meal, and I knew. I knew it was real. I knew I was awake."

And she had been afraid. But not of me.

She had been afraid of *waking up*.

"How did you know?" Varian asked. "Who told you that the fairy queen would also be forced to sleep? If the minstrels never mentioned that part . . ."

"My fairy godmother. She came to me when I was a child and explained everything. But she said I couldn't tell anyone, because if the fairy queen found out about her defiance, she would make sure the spell never worked." Rosalin blinked rapidly several times. "It's not like I had anyone to tell, anyhow. My father was determined to believe he had beaten the curse with his spinning wheel ban. Anytime I tried to suggest anything else, he told me I was imagining things, that he would take care of me and I didn't have to worry. I couldn't get anyone to listen to me. Who would have helped me?"

"I would have," I said quietly.

Rosalin turned to look at me. Her eyes were bright.

"I know you would have," she said. "Of course I do. Because in the end, Briony, you *did*."

16

*T*he spinning wheel stood in the center of the tower room.

I staggered away from the door, my breaths coming in harsh gasps. The wheel spun a notch, then stopped, waiting. Its bobbin was empty, the tip of the spindle shiny and sharp.

It was my sister's sixteenth birthday.

Don't you wish you could *try* spinning? You would probably be very good at it.

A whisper in my ear. Or in my memory? It felt like a memory, except I couldn't imagine where that memory might have come from.

The spinning wheel turned again, ever so slightly. As if pushed by wind, except there was no wind in that small round room.

As if it were extending an invitation.

"Sorry," I said out loud. "That doesn't seem like a good idea."

Then I turned and ran.

I pounded down the tower stairs, around and around, until I staggered to a stop against the door at the bottom. I waited to make sure I wasn't going to throw up, then pushed the door open and raced down the hallway. A flour-splattered servant scrambled out of my way as I turned into the main hall. Then the minstrel tried to stop me, his eyes bright and excited, but once I got away from him, there was no one between me and Rosalin's room.

I had to save Rosalin. Nothing else mattered.

She was alone, another surprise. A faint suspicion bloomed, somewhere far beneath my terror—it was as if someone had arranged for this to be easy. Then Rosalin turned to look at me, her dark eyes wide in her perfect face, and said, "Oh, really, Briony. Your hair looks like two gremlins have been using it for a weaving contest. If you need help with—"

I cut her off. "We have to get out of here."

She was on her feet instantly. "Why?"

"The curse," I panted. "There's—in the old watchtower—a spinning wheel."

Rosalin's face went white.

"Father's plan didn't work." I was almost incoherent, choking on sobs. "We have to leave the castle, Rosalin. We have to run. We have—"

"No," my sister said, and the clear coldness of her voice cut me into silence. "No. That's not what we need to do."

I could feel her terror, like an icy black fog; yet while my own fear made my legs quiver and my voice come apart, hers seemed only to sharpen and focus her.

I had never admired her so much, or felt more like she was the heroine of this story.

So when she said "Take me to the spinning wheel," I didn't argue.

———————◆———————

I blinked at my sister as if I had never seen her before.

"You knew the spinning wheel was there," I said. "You knew, because I told you!"

Rosalin shrank back.

"You knew," I repeated. I was so stunned I could barely get the words out. "You came to this room, you pricked your finger, on *purpose!*"

"I had to!" Rosalin said. "The fairy queen was coming after me. If I didn't put myself under my fairy godmother's spell, I was going to die." She leaned forward, her eyes fixed on me. "Don't you remember that part?"

———————◆———————

When we staggered into the tower room, the fairy godmother was waiting for us.

"Hurry," she said. Her wings were spread wide, catching the sunlight and making colored patterns dance on the walls of the room. "The queen is coming. I can't help you once she gets here!"

Rosalin's hand clutched mine so hard it hurt.

"You have to do this now," the fairy godmother said. "I cannot appear in the presence of my queen, not after defying her like this. She would kill me the second she saw me."

Rosalin wrested her hand free. Only then did I realize that I had been clinging to her, not the other way around.

"No!" I said shrilly. "Rosalin, don't. You can't. We have to find Mother and Father. We have to tell them—"

She walked away from me, taking slow, careful steps toward the spinning wheel.

"Don't!" I said. The word was swallowed in a sob. "Don't, Rosalin, please! I should never have told you about the spinning wheel! I should never have brought you here—"

"It's not your fault," Rosalin said without looking at me. "Don't feel guilty."

"I will feel guilty! Unless you stop."

Rosalin hesitated.

"She won't feel anything," the fairy godmother said to her. "I'll make your sister forget what happened this morning. She will have no recollection of her part in this."

In three quick strides, Rosalin covered the distance to the wheel. She placed one fingertip carefully on the spindle. She closed her eyes.

So she didn't see the wide, glittering smile that spread across her fairy godmother's face.

Terror arced through me, so intense I couldn't speak. Couldn't scream No!

A ruby-red globule swelled on my sister's finger, slow and tiny and bright.

And that was the last thing I saw for a very long time.

———◆———

I pressed my hand to my lips.

"I'm sorry," Rosalin said. "I'm *sorry*! You should never have been involved in this."

"Don't be ridiculous," I said. I had to speak around my sobs.

I had always been angry at Rosalin for not paying attention to me. But I was the one who hadn't been paying attention. I had never picked up on how scared she was. She had spent her entire life being afraid, and I'd had no idea how bad it was.

"*I'm* sorry," I said. "I would have helped you sooner if I'd known."

"I should have asked."

Well, *that* was true. But I shook my head.

"The past doesn't matter," I said. "Right now, we're trapped in this castle, and the fairy godmother is the only one who can help us get out. *And* the only one who knows where Edwin is. So we need to not make her angry." I sat back on the stool, reached for the wool hanging from the spinning wheel, and began pulling it thin.

"I won't be a part of this," Rosalin said. "I'm going to get Mother and Father."

"Rosalin," I said. "We have to work with your fairy godmother. We *have* to. She's the only one who can help us get out before . . . before . . ."

Before the Thornwood overcame us. Or before Rosalin died to stop it. I didn't know how to end that sentence, so I stopped.

"Not necessarily," Rosalin said. "There might be another way."

"Feel free to suggest one."

"Well, there's the royal wizard—"

I stared at my sister. She pressed her lips together.

"We'll figure something out," she said. "But get off that thing."

"You can't make me," I said.

Rosalin shook her head, turned, and stormed out of the room. Her footsteps thudded down the stairs.

Varian gave me an apologetic look, then went after her.

Every bone in my body wanted me to follow them. Instead, I positioned my feet on the pedals and began to spin.

This time, the spinning was even easier. The pedals moved smoothly up and down, and the wheel created a cool breeze against my face. The wool kept coming out of nowhere, rough between my fingers until the wheel pulled it tight. Gold whirred onto the bobbin, around and around, a shiny layer of magical thread.

It felt right. It felt like I had been meant to do this all along.

At least, it did until I got a cramp in my leg.

I kept going, but the steady burn in my muscles turned into a knot of agony. I whimpered and stopped. The bobbin was thickly layered with gold. That probably counted as full. At least, I hoped it did.

"What," I said aloud, "are you planning to do with this thread?"

"Exactly what you asked me to do," the fairy said from the window. "Hold off the Thornwood."

I turned, forgetting my precarious perch. I slid off the stool and landed on the floor, pitching forward onto my knees.

The fairy godmother laughed—a delicate, tinkling, annoyingly beautiful sound—and stepped lightly into the room. "There's no need to kneel before me, Princess. We are working together now."

I gritted my teeth and forced myself to my feet. I could feel my legs straining with a dull, painful ache, but I managed to stand.

"How is this thread going to help us fight the Thorn-wood?" I said.

"It's a magic spinning wheel, Princess. Anything that comes from it contains power. At its strongest, this wheel's thread could trap even the fairy queen." Her eyes glittered. "You just spun, instead of bleeding or dying, so it's not as much power as it could be. But it should be enough to hold the thorns back for a little while."

A little while. That didn't sound promising.

"How did the spinning wheel get here?" I asked.

She raised an eyebrow. "I brought it in. Did you think your father's ban would stop me?"

I felt a weird, guilty relief. Not that I'd ever truly thought it was anyone else, but . . . it was nice to *know* it wasn't. "How did you get it in without anyone seeing?"

She looked at me as if she couldn't believe anyone would ask such a stupid question. "Magic."

Right.

"That wheel is bursting with power," she went on. "Didn't you wonder how you managed to use it? It teaches people how to spin it. It could turn a novice into a master."

Or make someone who had never spun before feel like she had been doing it all her life.

"It cost me, too. I borrowed the spinning wheel from a friend, and he required quite the payment from me in return. I had to give him a new, secret name, and . . . Well, never mind. That's the last answer you'll trick out of me." She hopped backward onto the sill, wings an iridescent blur.

"I spun for you," I said quickly, before she could fly away. "Now take me to Edwin so I can see that he's all right. And then show me how we can get out of the castle."

The fairy smiled. She kept her lips shut over her teeth, so for a moment, she looked almost human. "Certainly. Come with me. I'll start by showing you where the Thornwood ends."

My heart hammered against my ribs. I knew, in my bones, that this was not going to end well.

But what choice did I have?

I took two steps to the window. The fairy's smile widened, revealing her teeth. She reached for me.

I had just enough time to think better of this—but not enough time to do anything about it—before she pulled me through the window.

17

The air rushed past my face. My feet dangled in the vast empty space between me and the thorns below. The tops of the trees quivered in the wind, a dark tangle of rough bark and shiny thorns.

I tried not to scream. What came out of my mouth instead was a cross between a squeak and a sob.

Above me, the fairy godmother laughed. "Where do you want to go, Princess?"

I forced myself to look up. Just enough to see where the Thornwood ended, where the red village rooftops and familiar rolling hills began.

But that wasn't what I saw.

The forest went on and on, as far as I could see, until its branches tangled with the dark blue of the horizon.

My breath froze in my chest.

"Back," I whispered. My small, weak voice was ripped away by the wind. "Back to the castle. *Please.*"

The fairy turned in midair, so suddenly that it felt like we were falling. I screamed and reached up, grabbing her wrists.

Then, when it was clear we *weren't* falling, I couldn't let go. I also couldn't pull air into my lungs.

The Thornwood unrolled below me, forever and ever and ever. It had no end. There was nothing at all on the other side of it. There *was* no other side.

We weren't barred from the village, from the world we had left. We had been ripped from that world and placed in the fairy realm. And there was nothing I could do to get back to the world where I belonged.

The fairy swooped low when we got to the castle. I squeezed my eyes shut—we were going too fast to make it through any of the windows; we were going to crash—

She let go of me, and I fell.

It was just a brief drop before I hit stone and rolled. I went on screaming for several seconds, even after I felt the solid stone below me, even after I opened my eyes and saw where we were: the rooftop. She had deposited me on the rough, flat surface between the battlements and a chimney.

She settled on one of the crenellations and crouched on it, her wings half shut.

"Are you *done?*" she asked when I paused for breath.

I thought about it. "Probably."

"Good. My ears are quite delicate."

I crossed my arms over my chest. "I'm only done because I need my breath for questions. You promised to show me where the Thornwood ends."

She smiled. "And now you know, don't you?"

I did know.

Nowhere. It never ended.

We'd had it all wrong. The Thornwood hadn't grown up around our castle. The Thornwood must have always existed, in the fairy realm, and our castle had been plunked down in the middle of it. There was no way we could ever cut through those trees.

And even if we did, there was nothing on the other side. No way back to the human world.

"How do we get out?" I said. "How do we get back where we belong?" I got to my feet. The rooftop around me was splattered with white specks of bird poop, and beyond the rooftop, gnarled brown branches stretched on and on. "How . . . how did you get Varian *in?*"

"Ah, yes. Prince Varian." She laughed. "Your sister's brave prince knows more about the fairies than he pretends. And more about the curse, too. You should ask *him* your questions."

That made sense. In the outside world, they'd had years and years to study our curse; everyone there probably knew more than we did.

But why wouldn't Varian have told us what he knew?

Unless it couldn't help us. Unless what he knew could only make things worse.

But he must have known where we were. He must have known the Thornwood was impassable. That we were in the fairy realm, that it was the *fairies* who . . .

All at once, I remembered Varian's amused expression when my sister and I were arguing over whose story this was. Now I knew what he had found so funny.

It wasn't either of our stories. It wasn't a human story at all.

"But it's not *our* curse," I said. "Is it?"

The fairy raised an eyebrow. "Clever girl."

A chill breeze whipped past, and I hunched my shoulders. "This spell isn't about *us*. It has nothing to do with Rosalin. She just got caught in it."

"Not quite." The fairy clicked her tongue. "Your sister isn't the *target* of the spell, true. But she is what made it work. When she pricked her finger, she set the spell in motion."

"Then who," I said, "was the spell's *target*? Who was it meant to put to sleep . . ."

My voice trailed off.

I would sleep for a hundred years, and so would the fairy queen.

"The fairy queen," I whispered. "This was an attack on *her*."

My fairy godmother smiled at me like my governess used to when I came up with a surprisingly good answer. "The castle had to be put to sleep so the Thornwood would sleep, so that the fairy queen inside the Thornwood would sleep. The spell had to be that roundabout or I couldn't have done it."

"Why did it have to happen at all?" I said. "Why couldn't you just leave her—and us—alone?"

"You don't know what you're saying, child. She is the *fairy queen*. She is vicious and vengeful and powerful. She wouldn't let the rest of us have any power, any freedom, at all."

"But what good did the spell do you? So you were free of her, for just a hundred years—"

I stopped talking even before she shook her head.

"Not for a hundred years," she said. "Forever."

I opened my mouth, then closed it.

"The story about the hundred years, and the prince..." The fairy shrugged. "That was just to pretty it up. To make your sister more inclined to go along with it. I needed her to prick her finger of her own free will, you see."

Rage rose in my throat, thick and sour. I pushed it down. There was no point. The fairy didn't care about my anger, or about me.

"And the story about the queen's original curse?" I said. "You made that up, too?"

She laughed. "As if the fairy queen would care about some petty human wedding! But when I told your parents she had cursed them, they believed me. And when their firstborn child was a girl, they were so scared for her that they were willing to listen to *anything* I said." Her smile widened, stretching so far across her face that she had no cheeks left. "And Rosalin was just as frightened. It was so easy to get her to prick her finger, to sacrifice herself and set my spell in motion. The queen was asleep before she had time to realize what was happening." She touched the side of her mouth, as if suddenly realizing it had grown too long, and stopped smiling. When she smirked, her mouth was normal sized. "And I was free, forever."

"But it wasn't forever," I said. "You woke us up, in the end. Why?"

"That wasn't me." Fury flashed across her face, just for a second; but a second was enough to remind me how dangerous she was. "That was your sister. She wouldn't stay asleep. She kept trying to wake up, dreaming of the princes I'd told her about. Eventually, she roused herself enough to break the spell on the queen … and then there was no turning it back."

"So Varian's kiss isn't what woke her?" I said.

The fairy shrugged. "She didn't really know she was

awake, I suspect, until he gave her a reason to open her eyes."

If I ever told the minstrel that line, he'd put it in at least three songs. I decided I would keep it to myself.

"Then why did you bring him here?" I asked.

She pursed her lips before speaking. "*That's* an answer you'll have to spin for."

"Some fairy godmother," I said.

She spread her wings. There was no sunlight hitting the roof, so they looked stark and black, shadows against the darkening sky. "The whole 'fairy godmother' concept is so useful. I'm really glad you humans thought it up."

I tried to think. "The fairy queen isn't defeated any longer, is she? She started waking up as soon as my sister woke. Now you need us to fight her for you."

The fairy hissed, a sound of pure rage and spite. In that moment, I saw how ridiculous it was that we had ever called this wild, vicious creature *godmother*.

My throat was dry with terror. But I went on. "You need our strength, and you need us to give it of our own free will. Our blood, our ... our energy. You need it for your spells. That's why you want me to spin. The fairy queen is coming for you, and you need *us*."

"You need me just as much," she said. "Our queen is ancient and cruel, and cares less for humans than even I do. She will kill everyone in this castle without a second thought. It is only my spell that keeps her in check."

"Your spell," I said, "and Rosalin's blood."

"Well, yes."

"So if Rosalin ..." I found it hard to say. "If Rosalin dies in the Thornwood ..."

"Then the queen will have that power, and she will break free. The Thornwood will vanish, and the rest of you will be free, too." She shrugged. "The queen might kill you all just because she feels like it. But she'll probably be too busy coming after me."

"So you *don't* want Rosalin to die?"

"Of course not. I saved her once already, didn't I? But we made a bargain, so I had to tell you the truth." The fairy raised a scornful eyebrow. "Besides, I don't think there's much risk that you'll try to act on that information."

I squeezed my eyes shut and opened them. "There has to be another way."

"I'm afraid there isn't. Not to get what *you* want. But I have a better idea." She rose into the air, wings an iridescent blur. "I think you'll like it. How do you feel about a ball?"

"A what?"

"It's quite appropriate." She turned in midair. "Especially since your sister never got to have her birthday party."

"What are you— Wait! What about Edwin?"

She looked at me over her shoulder, twisting her neck farther than any human could. "He's really not important, child. And you have time for only one more question. Think carefully about what it should be."

I gritted my teeth. *"Where. Is. He?"*

"If you must know, I put him in the second guest room in the west wing. I'm sure he's enjoying the luxury."

Then she turned and darted over the trees, disappearing into the dusky blue sky and leaving me alone on the roof.

18

From my vantage point on the top of the castle, I could see the old watchtower and the thorn branches clinging to it like dark, twisted ivy. They still hadn't reached the windows, but they were definitely higher than they had been before.

What I couldn't see, even after crisscrossing every inch of the roof, was any way to get back into the castle.

By now the sky was darkening, stripes of blue and purple streaking the horizon. It looked as if the Thornwood was pulling the sun down, swallowing its golden light. I wrapped my arms around my body as the air got colder, wedging myself against the side of the chimney, which was protection from the wind if nothing else. The stones weren't warm; there was no fire burning below. Whoever had the job of maintaining it must be in the distant village—no, they must be dead by now; they had lived their lives centuries ago, on the other side of the forest, in an entirely different world.

But there had to be a passage in the woods somewhere. A path between the two worlds that Varian had walked along. That we could also walk along, if we could only find it.

There is no other way, the fairy had said. Whatever path she had opened, it must already be gone, swallowed by the thorns.

But if she could open one, couldn't she open another?

Had I been bargaining for the wrong thing?

The sun dipped out of sight, leaving the sky a drifting mass of orange and pink clouds. I felt tears sliding down my cheeks, and since there was no one to see me, I made no effort to hold them back or even to wipe them away. They didn't stop until my eyelids slowly drooped shut over them.

I spun and spun, pedaled and pulled. I fed thorn branches into the spinning wheel, and the shiny black strands of Rosalin's hair came out around the bobbin.

"What are you doing?" My mother's face appeared in

fragmented flashes behind the whirring wheel. "Give your sister back her hair!"

"She'll never forgive you for this," Varian said behind me. "But she has me now. She doesn't need you."

I wanted to turn and face him, but I couldn't stop spinning. He grabbed my hair and yanked, and I screamed and—

———◆———

"Ouch!" Rosalin said. "Wake *up*, Briony!"

I jerked awake and yanked my hair free. At the same moment, I whirled and punched. Rosalin blocked the blow with the ease of long practice and grabbed my wrist.

"You have to come with us," she said. "There's something strange going on."

"Just one thing?" I managed to say. I forced my eyes all the way open. The moon was a white circle in the sky, casting enough light over the roof for me to see Rosalin crouched next to me. Varian was standing farther back. He had changed into fine hose and a velvet doublet.

My head felt like it was wrapped in fog, and my body was aching and cold. When I tried to stretch my legs, my calves spasmed with pain. "What— When— How did you find me?"

"Your place card," Rosalin explained, "said you were on the roof."

"My what?"

She sighed. "Come with us and you'll see."

———◆———

The way down from the roof, it turned out, was by a ladder that led to a balcony. The ladder was covered with thorn branches, but Varian slashed through them. He continued to chop them with one hand as he lowered himself off the roof. He landed on the balcony, whirled, and swung his sword in a wide arc, slicing through a jumble of grasping branches.

He was getting a lot better with his sword. I guess that's the benefit of intense practice while being attacked by evil trees.

Rosalin climbed down gingerly, hampered by her billowing skirt. When she stepped on her hem, she instinctively reached down to lift it, lost her balance, and tumbled straight into Varian's arms.

They both froze, so completely that for a moment I wondered if the spell had hit again and somehow turned them into statues.

Then Varian said in a low whisper, "Rosalin. I never should have lied to you."

Her lips parted, but she said nothing.

A thorn pricked my ankle, and I shrieked and jumped away. Varian and Rosalin both looked up.

"Sorry to interrupt," I said, "but I need to get down, too."

Varian obligingly hacked some branches away, and I jumped. I managed not to trip on my hem and fall into anyone's arms. Instead, I twisted my ankle when I landed on it, which made me stagger toward the balcony's railing and forced Varian to slice through some branches before their thorns could reach me.

"Are you all right?" he said.

I nodded. I felt a twinge in my ankle, but I could tell it wasn't serious.

Varian lunged forward and chopped through another set of branches while Rosalin and I hurried inside. Then he backed through the balcony doors and kicked them shut.

We found ourselves in an abandoned bedroom: chests of clothes stood open, a few pieces of jewelry were strewn on the bed, and two mismatched shoes had been flung into a corner. Someone else who had packed and gotten out before the spell hit and had lived their entire life hundreds of years ago, safe from fairies and their schemes.

As soon as Varian shut the door, Rosalin turned and led us out of the room.

I kind of hoped the two of them would hold hands

while we walked, but I wasn't really surprised when they didn't. I knew my sister, and I knew she held grudges.

But I also had a feeling she would forgive Varian eventually, just like she always ended up forgiving me.

I would have to find a moment to tell Varian that.

"Where are we going?" I said, hurrying after them.

"To the ball," Rosalin said.

"The what?"

"You'll see when we get there."

I stopped. "I can't go to a ball."

"I'm not in the mood, either," Rosalin said. "But we don't have a choice. Also, there's food there."

"I need to get Edwin," I said.

She blinked. "Didn't my fairy godmother say she was going to keep him safe?"

"Yes, and *she* certainly seems reliable."

"She can't lie," Varian said. "Not if she made a bargain. Didn't you spin for her in return?"

"Um . . ." I tried to recall the exact sequence of events that had led to me spinning, the fairy taking Edwin, and my flight over the endless Thornwood. "I think so. Sort of."

"Then you have nothing to worry about."

"I'm worried about *Edwin*! He's alone in this castle. He must be scared out of his mind."

"He's probably asleep," Varian said reassuringly.

Rosalin coughed. "That wouldn't stop him from being scared."

"If he wakes up," Varian said, "he'll come looking for us. And if he's asleep, he's probably safer than we are."

"Varian's right, Briony," Rosalin said. "We can't go chasing after him right now."

"You came chasing after *me*," I pointed out.

"That was different," Rosalin said. "He's not important."

"There's a whole castle full of people at stake," Varian added. "We can't waste time going after just one person."

"Oh, really?" I crossed my arms over my chest. "I believe the whole reason we're in this castle is because I was trying to save just one person."

In the silence that followed, a vine ripped through the tapestry behind us with a slow tearing sound. The vine stretched toward Rosalin, and she stepped away with barely a glance at it, her eyes glued to mine.

"Don't be stubborn," she said.

"Does that line ever work on *actually stubborn* people?" I turned away from them, my hands clenched at my sides. "I'm going to find him. I'll come to the ballroom after I do."

I was concentrating hard on not crying, so I didn't hear their footsteps until I started up the stairs. By then

Rosalin was already beside me, and Varian was only a step behind her.

"Well?" Rosalin said when I stopped and stared at her. "If you're going to insist on doing this, let's at least do it quickly."

I bit my lip so I wouldn't . . . smile at her? Snap at her? I wasn't sure which I wanted to do, but either seemed inappropriate. I looked straight ahead.

Together, the three of us strode up the stairs.

19

The west wing was the fanciest section of the palace, which was why most of the guest rooms were there. Lush blue rugs covered the hallway floors, and twisted iron chandeliers hung from the ceiling. One of the chandeliers had thorn branches wrapped grotesquely around it; they had forced their way through a crack in the ceiling, and now large, wicked thorns jutted in every direction. We all took care not to walk directly under it.

The door to the second guest room was shut. Rosalin raised a fist as if to knock, then hesitated and looked at me.

"I don't hear anything," she said. "Do you think he's . . ." She bit her lip. "Still asleep?"

"The fairy said she would keep him alive," I said, answering the question she had really been asking. "I'm sure he's fine."

Except of course, I wasn't sure. Which was why we

were all standing there staring at the door instead of pushing it open.

"We don't have time to waste," Varian said. Though *he* made no move to open the door, either.

Rosalin leaned forward, her shorn hair swinging across her cheek. "Wait. I do hear something."

"You're imagining it," I said. But a second later, I heard it, too: a low-pitched, melodic sound. It didn't sound like Edwin. It sounded like . . .

"With flawless skin and lustrous hair, a beauty quite beyond compare . . ."

"Are you *kidding* me?" I said, and pushed the door open.

The minstrel broke off mid-verse, lowering his lute. The terror on his face turned swiftly to relief when he saw me, and then to elation when he saw who was behind me.

"Princess Rosalin! Prince Varian!" He swept into a bow, hastily righting his lute after it swung up and hit the side of his forehead. "I have been searching for you!"

"Really?" Rosalin said. She swept her gaze around the room, from the canopied bed to the delicate wooden furniture. "In *here*?"

I ignored them. On the bed, resting against a pillow with a pitiful expression on his face, lay Edwin.

His face was clean and smooth, with no hint of the bruises that had been covering it when I'd seen him last.

His clothes were immaculate, and nicer than the ones he had been wearing—his silk doublet looked like it belonged to a nobleman—and there was no blood on them anywhere.

My first impulse was to rush to him, but if I did, I wasn't sure whether I would hug him or punch him. Since either would be embarrassing—in different ways—I played it safe by staying where I was.

"Why are you just lying there?" I demanded. "How long have you been awake?"

Edwin wiped one hand across his forehead, his fingers tangling in his hair—which, at the moment, actually looked worse than mine, tufts sticking out at improbable angles. "I was hoping you could tell me. Last thing I remember, we were in the Thornwood, and the branches were growing over me and pulling me down. . . ." He shuddered, and I stopped feeling gleeful about his hair. "Next thing I knew, I woke up in this bed, and the minstrel was asking me for opinions about this song he's composing."

"I have been waiting for him to wake ever since I discovered him," the minstrel announced. "I was hoping he could give me details, to make the song more authentic. The chorus is going to be about how Prince Varian fought his way through the thorns and vanquished the Thornwood forever."

Edwin looked pointedly up. I followed his gaze and saw that, in the corner of the ceiling right above him, a gnarled branch had squeezed through a crack and was spreading slowly, its thorns sticking into the ceiling and causing more cracks to spiderweb along the white paint.

"He has been most unhelpful," the minstrel sighed. He turned to Varian. "Nevertheless, I've perfected a *transcendent* stanza about how you saved your lady love from the thorns after she foolishly ventured out into them. If you want to hear it—"

"NO," we all said in unison.

"That's not even what happened," I added. "It wasn't Varian who saved us. It was my sister's fairy godmother."

The minstrel frowned. "Are you sure?"

"Yes, I'm sure. I was there!"

His brow furrowed. "Why were *you* there?"

I turned away. "Edwin, come on. We have to go to a ball."

Edwin transferred his gaze from the thorn branch to me. "A . . . what?"

"You've missed a few things," I said. "I'll explain on the way."

———◆———

It turned out that *explain* was a bit of an exaggeration. I was able to fill Edwin in on what had happened since our disastrous attempt to fight the Thornwood. I had a bit more trouble explaining *why* any of it had happened, what it meant, or how we were going to deal with it.

Luckily, the minstrel had decided to stay behind and "get his song ready for the ball," so I was able to speak freely as we walked through the corridors. Rosalin and Varian walked a few steps ahead of us, talking in low tones. At one point, Varian started to reach for Rosalin's hand, then stopped before she noticed. Probably wise, even though I thought there was about a fifty percent chance she wouldn't have pulled away. I recognized the signs of my sister getting over a snit.

"So," Edwin said, "the whole spell was really designed by the fairy godmother to put the fairy queen to sleep? And now that your sister is awake, the fairy queen is also awake and is probably going to kill us all?"

"Well," I said. "Yes. But it's not as bad as it sounds, because . . . um . . ."

". . . because the fairy godmother who made this happen in the first place has now promised that she can save us?"

"Well, no," I said. "She didn't actually promise anything."

Edwin groaned. "I think I liked the minstrel's version better."

"Sorry," I said. "Would you prefer to have been left there with him?"

"Tough call." Edwin chewed the side of his lip. "That bed was *very* comfortable."

"I'm sure it was," I said. "But we need you."

His eyes widened, and I noticed for the first time that they were the gray-blue color of the sky right after sunrise. He looked like I had just handed him an unexpected gift.

It made me uncomfortable, so I raised my eyebrows at him. "You *have* proved yourself useful in the past. Just try to rescue the right princess this time."

Edwin kept looking at me, with no change in his expression. "I think I rescued the right princess already."

A warm feeling rose in my throat. "Well. It's good to have some variety."

As we passed one of the large rectangular windows, the velvet curtains jutted out and a thorn-covered branch slid between them and reached in our direction. I jumped away and quickened my pace, hearing fabric rip behind me.

"I'm sorry," I said.

Edwin blinked. "For what?"

"For getting you into this."

"You didn't get me into anything," Edwin pointed out.

"I'm the only person in the castle who *wanted* to be here. Well, me and the minstrel, I guess. I have no reason to be angry at anyone."

I let out a breath, surprised at how relieved I felt. But I've never been very good at knowing when to let things go. "You chose to be here so that after a hundred years you could go back to a village full of people who didn't know you. I don't think your goal was to end up trapped in the Thornwood and stuck in the middle of some kind of fairy war."

"No," he admitted. "I didn't anticipate that. But, you know. People who walk into enchanted castles have no right to expect things to go according to plan."

"Aren't you scared?" I said.

"I'm used to being scared. I'm always scared." Something dark flickered on his face. "Fear is like any other bad emotion. It settles in your gut like a rock, and you work around it."

But my fear didn't feel like a rock. It was a quiver running through me, a weakness that had taken over my body from the inside.

Edwin reached for my hand, squeezed it, and let go. "It will be all right," he said. "You bargained with the fairy to save me, and I'll . . . I'll find a way to save you, too. As long as we work together, I think we'll get out before it's too late. Don't you?"

I avoided his gaze, watching the thorny vines wind along the walls. Now my fear was mingled with guilt, because I still hadn't told Edwin the whole truth. Nobody knew what the fairy had told me, about the way we *could* all get out of here.

The human who can make the Thornwood stop is your sister. And the way she can stop it is by dying in it.

I couldn't tell him. I couldn't tell anyone. The people here already blamed Rosalin for trapping us in the castle. If they knew that her death could save us all . . .

Because the thing was, they were right. We had done this to them. We had been scared, so we had done the only thing we could to save Rosalin's life. We had gone to that room with the spinning wheel, knowing what would happen.

Had we even thought about anyone but ourselves?

We had acted like this was our story. Like the other people in it—everyone in this castle, and outside it, too— were minor details we didn't have to pay attention to.

I had been so angry at Rosalin for thinking of me that way. But I was no better.

And as we walked down the hall, our footsteps thudding on the rug, I found that I had no answer to Edwin's question.

20

We walked into the entrance hall and stopped short.

The Thornwood had spread across the front wall like a grotesque, deadly decoration. One branch had dislodged the portrait of my great-grandfather King Sigamond the Brave, leaving it hanging lopsided from one corner. King Sigamond looked annoyed, though to be fair, he had looked that way even when the portrait was straight.

"They're growing faster," I said.

"Indeed," Varian said grimly, "they are." He turned into the ballroom.

The rest of us followed him through the doorway. Then, once again, I stopped.

The room was dazzling. All the chandeliers were lit, illuminating tables laid with gold-embroidered cloths and covered with food. The feast was an odd mix of noble and peasant fare, as if put together by someone who didn't know the difference: meat pies, roast chicken, and fried eel sat on platters together with wedges of cheese and steaming bowls of vegetable stew.

The smell made my stomach rumble loudly. I hadn't eaten since the blueberry muffin in the sitting room.

Most of the chairs were empty. Our ballroom could seat hundreds, but only three of the long rectangular tables were full. One held a collection of ladies-in-waiting, and the other two were occupied by a motley collection of servants, maids, and members of the lower nobility.

My heart sank. I hadn't realized just how few people were left in the castle.

Of course, for all I knew, the rest were hiding away in their rooms instead of attending . . . whatever this was.

There was one round table at the far end of the room. My parents were seated at it, so busy eating they hadn't yet noticed our presence.

"What is this?" I asked.

"It seems," Rosalin said, "that my fairy godmother has decided to throw me a birthday party."

Her voice was a little too loud, and everyone looked at us, including our parents. My mother's eyes lit up when she saw us, and my father gestured us over.

"Right," I said. "And we've all decided to just . . . go along with it?"

"Not at first," Varian said. "You missed all the shock and gasping and wild speculation. But, you know." He shrugged. "Everyone's hungry."

That was definitely true. I inhaled the smell of roast meat and fresh bread, and my stomach let out an embarrassingly loud growl. Even as my mind told me this was a bad idea, my feet followed Rosalin and Varian to my parents' table with its three empty chairs.

Three empty chairs. I glanced back at Edwin. But he had already pulled out a chair between two servants and was shoveling dumplings into his mouth. I guessed he wasn't insulted.

Or maybe he was just too hungry to care. Just like I was. Just like everyone in this castle was, after a whole day without food.

Which meant this *was* everyone left in the castle—or almost everyone. There couldn't be many who could resist the promise of a banquet.

It was all I could do to maintain a dignified pace as I followed Rosalin and Varian across the room. As soon as we reached the table, I grabbed a meat pastry and bit into it. I was halfway through it before I realized it was mutton. I hated mutton.

I didn't care. Maybe it was fairy magic, or maybe it was hunger, but *this* mutton was delicious. I gobbled the rest down, drained my water—which was flavored with lemon, something else I normally hated—and cut myself a huge slice of pheasant pie.

Beside me, Rosalin was eating just as voraciously, though somehow she managed to look dainty doing it. Varian, on the other hand, was taking his time, cutting his chicken into evenly sized bites. My parents watched us with the slightly sick expressions of people who have eaten too much too fast and are waiting for the food to settle so they can eat more.

On the wall behind them, a thorn-studded vine had curved around the edge of a large tapestry and was snaking toward the floor.

"Don't overeat," my father warned. "This would not be a good time to get a stomachache. We still don't know exactly what's going on, or how the fairy godmother is going to help us."

I spoke around a chunk of pie. "*Help* us?"

"Well," my mother said, "she has prepared this entire banquet. Obviously, she is kindly disposed toward us, and is going to release us from the spell. I'm sure she'll come soon to explain."

I snorted. Unfortunately, since my mouth was full of pie, my snort came with a spray of crumbs. My mother winced. I grabbed a linen napkin and swiped at my lips. In the process, I knocked over the neat placard propped up next to my plate. I picked it up.

Sleeping Beauty's Wake-Up Party! pronounced glittering gold letters on the front. *Hosted by her fairy godmother.*

I flipped it open to read the inside.

Princess Briony. Table 1.
Please retrieve the princess from the rooftop.

I reached over and picked up Rosalin's place card. She narrowed her eyes as if about to object, but her mouth was too full for her to say anything.

The outside of her card was the same as mine. The inside read:

Sleeping Beauty. Guest of Honor.

Well, that would make the minstrel happy.

I ate another slice of pie and glanced at Edwin. He seemed to fit right in at the servants' table. He was laughing with another boy.

The pie lodged in my throat. *Good for him,* I told myself, but my throat still felt thick. It reminded me of watching the kitchen girls, joking and easy with each other; of the way they had gone sedate and guarded whenever I approached. Their careful smiles when I joined them, and they had to pretend to be my friends.

I swallowed my pie and focused on my mother. Her

face was, as always, composed and calm. But there was a tiny bit of sauce on the tip of her chin. That was the equivalent of anyone else having a full-fledged panic attack.

"I'm not sure," I said carefully, "that we can count on the fairy godmother." Which was an understatement, but the last thing I needed was for my mother to have an *actual* panic attack.

"Of course not," my father said. He looked and sounded dreadfully tired. "Fairies are notoriously unpredictable. But your mother is right. This banquet is a good sign."

"And the royal wizard," my mother said, "is working on a spell. Between the two of them, we'll be out of here by morning."

I looked down at my plate. I could hardly blame my mother. She came from a long line of royalty, and in her family, princesses were *rescued*. My father had failed to rescue us with his spinning-wheel ban, so now she needed to believe someone else would take care of us. A prince with a sword. The royal wizard. The fairy god-mother.

But no one was coming. The only thing coming for us was the Thornwood, and it was going to keep coming, worming its way into the castle, climbing and stabbing and strangling. And no one—*no* one—knew how to stop it.

Varian and Rosalin had pulled their chairs close together, and they were exchanging whispers as they ate. I heard a snatch from Varian—"the stories didn't say you were also brave"—and saw a blush creep up Rosalin's cheeks.

I knew my sister. Not as well as I'd thought, maybe, but we had grown up in this castle together. I knew that the one part of her story she had always loved was the end, when her prince came for her.

Even if Varian wasn't a prince, I knew she was falling in love with him.

And Varian? He watched her with a surprised respect. I had seen it first in the Thornwood, when he'd realized how scared and how brave she was, and it had been growing ever since. He leaned close when she spoke, his expression hopeful. I suspected he was falling in love, too.

You should ask him *your questions. He knows more about the fairies than he pretends.*

But why should I believe the fairy? What if she had simply intended to sow discord among us? To keep us from working together to figure out our own way out of the castle?

Across the table, my parents were also conversing in low tones. (I caught the words *royal wizard* a lot.) I was the only one who had no one to talk to.

I looked over at the servants' table again and was surprised to meet Edwin's gaze. He jerked his head toward the door, as if indicating that he wanted to meet me outside the ballroom.

I suddenly felt lighter, despite the food sitting like lead in my stomach. I put my napkin down. "May I be excused?"

"I don't think that's a good idea," my mother said.

"But I have to clean my face," I said.

"And fix your hair," Rosalin added. "You look like a Pegasus caught in a windstorm."

She flashed me a grin. I didn't grin back.

"Very well," my mother said. "But please be quick. We don't want to insult Rosalin's fairy godmother by not being here when she arrives."

The food I had just eaten roiled in my stomach. *I have a better idea*, the fairy had said on the rooftop. Whatever that idea was, she had staged this ball to announce it to us.

But was it a better idea for us? Or just better for *her*?

"I'm sure she'll be here soon." My mother looked around the glittering, mostly empty room. Her gaze paused briefly on the far wall, where a thorny branch had grown through a crack in the stones and was reaching into the room with gnarled, fingerlike twigs. Her hand trembled, and she put her fork down. "I can't wait to hear what she has planned."

There was no point in arguing with my mother, so I didn't. But I knew, deep down, that putting ourselves in the fairy's hands was a terrible idea. She didn't care about us; she only cared about how she could use us to fight her battle with the queen. She would do everything she could to keep us trapped here so her queen couldn't get free.

The only way we could escape was to outwit her and force her to help us.

And since I couldn't think of any way to do that, I very much hoped Edwin had a plan in mind.

21

I folded my napkin, put it next to my plate, and twisted again to look at the servants' table. But Edwin was no longer watching me. Instead, he was leaning over a platter of roast duck, listening intently as one of the page boys spoke.

My throat tightened. But just as I was about to turn back to my own table, Edwin glanced up and caught my eye. I half-rose, and he grinned and swung his legs to the side of his chair.

A clash of cymbals rang through the hall, and I jumped. A moment later, it was joined by the quick, high strains of a fiddle, and then the gentle, layered melody of a harp. I sat back down and looked around, but there were no musicians, no instruments. The music was coming from nowhere.

It was a dancing tune, lively and urgent. Even before

my heartbeat slowed, I caught myself tapping my foot against the floor.

Varian put his knife down, stood, and held his hand out to Rosalin. His fingers were long and slender, his skin smooth and unbroken. How had his scratches healed so fast?

Rosalin crammed the last of her bread into her mouth, swallowed, and burped. I giggled. My mother glared at me, but Rosalin shot me a conspiratorial look as she dabbed her lips with a napkin.

Varian waited, his hand trembling slightly. He looked so hopeful that I nudged Rosalin under the table.

"My lady," Varian said. "I know I don't deserve it. But I would . . . I would be honored if you would join me in a dance."

Rosalin looked up at him. For a long moment they stared at each other, like they were committing each other's eye color to memory. It was probably very romantic for them, but it was awkward for the rest of us. I looked down at my plate. My father coughed. My mother kept watching the thorn branch across the room, which seemed to have grown in the past few minutes.

"My prince," Rosalin said finally, and slid her hand into his. "Of course I'll dance with you."

Varian's eyes widened. Then he smiled, and for some

reason, I felt tears coming to my eyes. I blinked them back as Rosalin let Varian draw her to her feet.

For a moment, I thought they were going to kiss yet again. I shifted my eyes to Varian's plate, which was still covered by small, perfectly square pieces of chicken.

Wow. He really must have been in love, if he preferred dancing with Rosalin to eating. I mean, that was the kind of thing the minstrel always said when he wrote poems about her—"your beauty is all the sustenance I need," "your voice is sweeter than wine," blah blah blah—but I suspected the minstrel was never *hungry* when he wrote those lines.

The music got faster as Varian led Rosalin to the dance floor. He bowed, she curtsied, and they began to dance.

They passed the windows, and the curtains rippled and billowed, bulging in unnaturally sharp lumps. A shudder ran through me. There was a wall of thorns seething behind those thick curtains, pushing their way in.

The two dancers didn't seem to notice. They moved around the polished floor, all rustling silk and elegant velvet, as if they were the only two people in the room. Rosalin danced beautifully, and Varian did pretty well for a commoner. He clearly didn't know any of the steps, but he moved with surety, following the rhythm of the music. There was something oddly familiar about the way he danced, about his light, easy grace.

I knew the steps—I had spent hours every week practicing with a dancing tutor—but though the music thrummed through my bones, I knew it wasn't meant for me. It was all for Rosalin.

"My lady," someone said behind me, and I turned. Edwin stood behind my chair, a smear of grease on his cheek. He bowed awkwardly. "May I have this dance?"

My parents drew themselves up in sync and glared at him. Edwin flinched.

I hesitated for only a second. Then I pushed my chair back with a loud scrape.

"You may," I said.

I didn't dare look at my parents as I followed Edwin onto the dance floor. When we faced each other, I saw that his cheeks were flaming red.

"I, um," he said. "I don't actually know how to dance."

"Neither does Varian," I reassured him.

We glanced over at the pair, who were gliding around the room staring rapturously into each other's eyes. Behind them, another thorn branch squeezed through a crack in the walls, reaching for Rosalin. Varian whirled her away from it.

"Yeah," Edwin said. "But I think he might have some natural talent. I definitely don't."

"Then why," I said, "did you ask me to dance?"

"Because we need to talk." He reached for my hands, and we stepped sideways in time with the music.

Well, *I* stepped in time with the music. Edwin had not been exaggerating: he had zero talent for dancing.

"Ouch," I said when he stepped on my foot. Then "Urk" as he stepped back when he should have stepped forward, and almost pulled my arm out of its socket.

The music changed tempo, and we turned in a slow circle. Something bumped against my foot, almost making me trip. I looked down to see a thorn branch working its way through a space between the flagstones. My stomach lurched, and I swung us farther away from it.

"What do you need to tell me?" I asked.

Edwin leaned closer, accidentally slamming his forehead into mine. I ignored the thudding pain. Edwin kept his voice low. "The minstrel said . . . I'm sorry, Briony, but he told me that—"

The music came to an abrupt stop. In the sudden silence, we all heard Rosalin say "Because I love you."

She and Varian froze. Rosalin blushed so brightly I couldn't help but feel sorry for her, even if she *should* have been embarrassed, proclaiming herself in love with someone she'd known for only a day.

Then again, it had been an intense day.

The music started up again, but it wasn't a dance tune

this time. It was slow and plaintive, like a half-asleep melody.

The doors to the kitchen swung open and a cart rolled out. Rosalin's birthday cake teetered on top of it.

There was no one holding the doors open, and there was no one pushing the cart. It moved entirely by itself, past the table where my parents sat with their mouths hanging open, and creaked to a stop beside Rosalin and Varian.

The hole I had gouged in the side of the cake had been covered with frosting. It wasn't a great patch—the pastry chef was gone, obviously, and whoever had taken on the job had sloppily spread frosting in an uneven clump that didn't match the delicate whirls and lines on the rest of the cake—but it still looked better than it had in the kitchen.

The silence was absolute. Rosalin stared at the cake, her face white. I looked at the patch where I had ruined the cake and felt *my* face go red.

Honestly. Would it have been so hard for the fairy to do a better job of fixing that?

Varian grinned. He did it well—his smile looked easy and natural, like he was not at all bothered by a half-ruined birthday cake that moved around on its own. He reached into the cart and pulled out a fork.

"Happy birthday," he said. With an awkward jab I

found familiar—apparently, he was as unused to forks as he was to swords—he scooped up a chunk of frosting-laden cake and held it out to Rosalin. "To new beginnings, and to us."

Rosalin put one hand over her mouth.

"I—I can't," she said. "I want a new beginning with you. I do. But I can't eat anymore. I'm afraid I might throw up."

Varian looked stunned. Then he recovered and summoned up a smile—not nearly as convincing this time; it looked like it had been pasted onto his face. "Then allow me," he said, and took a bite—mainly of frosting. He chewed, swallowed, and tried the smile again. "It is as sweet as you are."

I refrained from rolling my eyes.

"As sweet," Varian went on, raising his voice for the rest of the room (not that they hadn't been hanging on every word until now), "as our lives together will be. Once we vanquish the remnants of this curse and free ourselves of the Thorn—"

He gagged on the word. His eyes went wide.

He fell over sideways, straight as a log. The fork with its remnant of cake flew out of his hand, skittered across the dance floor, and came to a clinking stop.

Varian lay flat on the floor, his arm stretched out, his body limp and motionless.

22

Rosalin screamed and threw herself onto Varian, grabbing his hands. His head lolled to one side. His eyes were closed, and his mouth drooped open.

"Varian! My love!" My sister knelt and pressed her cheek to his chest. "I need you. Please, please, wake up!"

Wake up . . . And she had her ear pressed to his chest. Did that mean she could hear his heart beating?

Either that or she was hysterical and not paying attention to reality. Still, there was at least a fifty percent chance that he was only sleeping.

Not that there was anything *only* about sleeping. Not in this castle.

I started toward them, but Edwin's grip on my hand yanked me back. I gave him an annoyed look and pulled free. He grabbed my wrist.

"We need to talk," he hissed.

"Not now!"

"Especially now! Don't you understand? That poison was meant for Rosalin!"

I stared at Edwin, then at Varian's unmoving body. Rosalin wept, her ragged hair falling over her cheeks, doing nothing to hide her anguished expression. On the floor a few feet away from her, a flagstone cracked, and the tip of a thorn branch broke through.

I replayed the last minute in my mind. Varian biting into the frosting. Chewing. Swallowing. And then, just seconds later—

Bile rose into my throat, sharp and sour.

"But *I* ate the cake," I said. "You saw me."

"The poison must have been added afterward. Spread on the frosting, probably."

"By *who*?"

"Anyone here. The servants. The castle staff. I'm sorry, Briony, but they hate your sister. They blame her for what happened to them."

"But—" My eyes went back to the gash in the cake. *I* had blamed Rosalin, too.

And that was even before I had known it was her fault. No. *Our* fault.

Rosalin raised her head, tears streaming down her cheeks. "Help me!"

My father got to his feet. My mother grabbed his hand

to hold him back. The thorn branch jutting from the ground crept sideways toward Rosalin's foot.

I shook free of Edwin's grip, ran across the ballroom, and dropped to my knees next to my sister.

This close, it was clear that Varian was breathing. His chest rose and fell evenly. I was surprised by how relieved I felt.

"Perhaps," a voice said from above, "we should have skipped dessert."

I looked up.

The fairy hovered above the cake, translucent wings spread wide. She looked around the ballroom, taking in the gaping faces and the utter silence.

"Tell me," she said. "Did you enjoy my feast?"

Nobody moved.

"If you're finished eating," she added, "you may leave."

There was a sudden clatter of chairs and a thunder of feet. Within thirty seconds, the ballroom was empty except for me and Rosalin, my parents at their table— and Edwin, still standing where I had left him.

I felt a surge of gratitude. I tried to catch Edwin's eye, but he was staring at the fairy hovering above me.

"The food was delicious, wasn't it?" the fairy went on. "I went a little lighter on the spices than I would have preferred. But I figured, when you're cooking for a crowd . . ."

"Why?" Rosalin interrupted her. "Why did you do all this?"

The fairy's yellow eyes went wide. "I did it for you! I am your fairy godmother, after all."

Rosalin clenched her fists. "What do you want from us?"

"I simply want you to be safe." The fairy gestured at the remnants of the feast—or maybe at the haphazardly knocked-over chairs; it was hard to tell. "And as I have demonstrated, I can keep you safe. I can maintain you in this castle while you are awake, just as I did when you were asleep. I can give you everything you need to live and be happy."

The thorn branch touched Rosalin's toe. The fairy glanced down and waved her hand, and the branch froze, though its tips writhed angrily.

"Can you wake him up?" Rosalin asked.

The fairy blinked at her. "I could do that, yes. Are you sure you want me to?"

"Of course I'm sure!" Rosalin lifted her chin. "I love him."

"Do you? Even after he told you the truth about himself? How unexpectedly broad-minded of you."

"I don't care what he is," Rosalin said. "He's still the man who saved me. And nobody deserves to sleep forever."

"It's better than being dead," the fairy said. Her voice went oddly gentle. "Isn't it?"

Rosalin hid her face in her hands. When it became evident that she wasn't going to reply, I said, "*Would* he be dead? Was the poison meant to kill"—I swallowed—"to kill whoever ate it?"

"It was quite deadly," the fairy said. "It would kill most humans in a heartbeat."

"Who did it?" I asked. My voice shook.

The fairy shrugged. "There are many angry people in this castle. But you don't have to worry about them. I will not allow death to befall anyone under my protection. No death, no illness, no old age. You will all be safe and happy and have everything your hearts desire, *forever*."

"I won't have everything my heart desires," Rosalin said, "if I don't have him."

The fairy sighed. "You are missing the point."

I couldn't help but agree. "So *this* is your great idea?" I said to the fairy. "To keep us here forever? That's not what we want."

"I've told you," she answered. "The power within the Thornwood is the power of my queen, and it is far stronger than I. I cannot vanquish it. I can only hold it off."

Or maybe she didn't *want* to vanquish it. She wanted us to stay trapped here. Because that way, the fairy queen would be trapped here, too.

I glanced again at the branches clinging to the walls. There were more of them now—almost a dozen—and they were spreading from the ceiling like a gnarled, angry tapestry.

"What do you want from us in return?" I said.

"Nothing," the fairy said. "I will only need your help to keep the Thornwood from creeping into your walls."

"You want us," I said, "to spin."

My mother gasped.

The fairy smiled. "The spinning wheel in the tower is ancient and powerful. With human strength poured into it, it can hold off the Thornwood." She turned to Rosalin. "And you shall have gold thread, too. Enough to wear golden dresses, to sleep beneath golden sheets. The minstrel can call you the Golden Princess."

Rosalin shrank back.

"Or perhaps not." The fairy shrugged and rose higher into the air, her hair floating around her inhuman face. "Everything that comes from that spinning wheel repels the Thornwood. Working together, we can harness its power and keep you safe."

"Keep *you* safe," I said. "That's all you really care about."

The fairy looked at me. Her eyes had turned black. "But I have to keep you safe in order to keep myself safe. That's all *you* should care about."

"All right," Rosalin said.

"What?" I said. "No! We're not staying here. We need to use the spinning wheel's power to get *out*."

"That is not what will get you out," the fairy said.

The warning was clear: *Be quiet, or I will tell everyone how you can really get out.*

Everyone. Including the people who hated Rosalin. It would seem perfectly fair to them: She had gotten them into this; her death could get them out of it. If the fairy told them the truth, there was no way I would be able to stop them.

Of course, the fairy didn't want them to know the truth, either. Did I dare call her bluff?

I shut my mouth.

Rosalin stepped toward the fairy. Her hair hung unevenly around her face, her eyes were puffy, and her cheeks were streaked with the remnants of her tears. She was still beautiful beyond belief. "Prove that you can do what you say. If you can save us, save *him*."

The fairy sighed. "You will have your prince." She tilted her head. "Although I would prefer that you not tell him about my . . . generosity."

"Why not?" Edwin demanded.

"He's a hero." There was an odd note in her voice—a sullen sort of fear. Then her lip curled contemptuously, and I was sure I had imagined her reaction. Why would the fairy be afraid of Varian when she had *chosen* him to come here? "Heroes are not very good at being practical."

She sank to the floor and considered Varian's still form. One corner of her mouth twitched. She extended her leg, gracefully and disdainfully, and nudged him in the side with her toe.

"When you decide to accept my offer," she said, "come spin for me."

Then she vanished.

Varian groaned and sat up, looking puzzled. He glanced around the near-empty ballroom. "What happ—"

Rosalin launched herself at him, threw her arms around his neck, and burst into tears.

At that moment, the main doors banged open and the royal wizard strode into the ballroom.

"I am here!" he shouted, spreading his arms wide. "I sensed the magic in this room and came to answer your summons! Command me, Your Majesties, and I will defend you!"

The ballroom went absolutely silent.

The royal wizard did not look particularly imposing. His eyes were puffy, his hat was askew, and his cape (gold and purple) didn't match his clothes (red and white). There was also a distinct . . . smell to him.

My mother rose to her feet, hands clasped. "You came!"

"I always come," the royal wizard said grandly, "when

I am needed." He looked around the room and frowned. "Did I miss the food?"

Before anyone could answer, he lurched to one of the tables, grabbed a half-eaten drumstick off an abandoned plate, and bit into it.

"Well," Edwin said to me in a low voice, "I guess we know where the wine from the apothecary went."

My father had come to the same conclusion. He stood up next to my mother. "Are you *drunk?*" he demanded of the wizard.

"It only ... appears ... that I am," the royal wizard said between bites. He tossed the bone aside and grabbed a roll. "I have been working great and terrible magics to figure out a way to release us from our plight. I had to partake of wine so I could access the depths of . . . um . . ." He closed his eyes. "This is the best bread I have ever tasted."

My parents looked at each other uncertainly.

"No offense to the royal baker! Not his fault. It's fairy food. They have magic. Unfair advantage." He burped, then held up an index finger. "We must make a law, Your Majesties, that fairies may not enter baking competitions."

"Sir Wizard," my father said carefully, "we are in great peril."

"I know. I know! And only I can save you." He looked

around the table. "Fortunately for you, I am the type of wizard whose casual sloppiness disguises great power and awe-inspiring wisdom. I have discovered the answer to our dilemma. Meet me in my workshop!"

He grabbed a slice of pie and snapped his fingers. There was a boom, and he was surrounded by thick purple smoke that smelled even worse than he had.

When the smoke dissipated, it revealed the royal wizard still standing there, halfway through the slice of pie.

"Oh, *bother*," he said. Crumbs sprayed from his mouth. "There are forces at work fighting my magic. But I know what needs to be done. I will persevere, no matter the cost!"

He plucked a handful of nuts from the table and strode out of the room.

A few tendrils of purple smoke drifted toward me. I coughed and waved them away.

My parents dashed around the table and followed the royal wizard out the door.

"Wait!" I said.

Needless to say, they ignored me.

"Stay here!" my mother called over her shoulder.

"Just wait quietly," my father added. "Don't be afraid! We'll save you."

They ran through the door, and we heard their footsteps pound down the hall and then fade into silence.

23

Varian got slowly to his feet. His face twisted in pain.

"My love!" Rosalin said, turning quickly back to him. "Are you all right?"

"Yes. But I . . ." He looked down at her. "What happened?"

"My fairy godmother. She . . ." Rosalin hesitated. "She offered us a bargain."

"Right," I said. "So I guess we're telling him, then."

"Telling me what?" Varian said. "And why *wouldn't* you tell me?"

Rosalin lowered her voice, even though the four of us were the only ones left in the ballroom. "The fairy said not to tell you that she offered us a deal. She said she'll keep us safe and comfortable in the castle, and in return, we have to spin for her. Our spinning will give her the strength she needs to keep the Thornwood at bay."

"Hmm." Varian's eyes narrowed. "You think she can do it?"

"Fairies always keep their bargains," Rosalin said.

"It may not be in her power to keep this one. The fairy queen is far stronger than she is."

"But not stronger than all of us together," Edwin said. "If we spin for her and give her our strength, she can protect us. She couldn't have offered the bargain if that weren't true."

"You can't be serious!" I said. "You're really thinking about saying yes?"

Their silence was my answer.

"We can't trust the fairy!" I protested. "Why do you think she suggested this? There must be something in it for her. We have no idea what she really wants."

"I think," Varian said slowly, "she's afraid."

"Of the fairy queen?" Rosalin said. "Then why doesn't she *run* instead of staying here with us?"

"She can't run from her queen. And even if she could . . ." Varian let out a breath. "The human world doesn't have much space for fairies anymore. In the centuries that you've been gone, it's been taken over by machines and metal. The magic has been . . . leached out of it." His voice was heavy. "The fairies in my world hide, and do their best to keep humans from knowing they exist. They don't get invited to balls. They don't perform grand spells. They are heard of mostly in stories, and the majority of people—even the ones who come to see the Thornwood—don't believe that those stories are true."

He turned his head away, blinking as if to hold back tears.

"Then how do *you* know they exist?" I asked.

"Well," Varian said, "one of them gave me a magic sword. So that was very convincing."

Which made sense. But there was something too smooth about the way he said it.

He knows more about the fairies than he pretends.

"Enough," Rosalin said. She took Varian's hand. He looked at her, and she said, "When I saw you fall . . . when I thought you were . . . Oh, Varian. I'm sorry. It doesn't matter to me what you are."

Varian's lips curved into a smile. "Good," he murmured, and they bent their heads together.

Oh, great.

I looked pointedly away and caught Edwin doing the same. We both snickered. I jerked my head sideways and the two of us walked toward the tables.

In the corner, the flagstones were bulging. I examined the floor carefully—there were no branches getting through here, not yet—then looked up at Edwin.

"What were you going to tell me?" I asked.

He jerked his gaze from a slice of pecan pie. "What?"

"Before the music stopped. You said the minstrel told you something. What was it?"

He swallowed. "It's . . . about your bird."

"Twirtle? What does the minstrel—"

And then I remembered the first stanza the minstrel had sung, back when we had faced each other outside my sister's room: *Though all the birds and beasts have fled . . .*

And the kennel boy: *Someone unlocked the kennel gate, and there was no stopping them.*

"He let them out," I said. My voice echoed hollowly, so loud that across the room, Rosalin and Varian stopped with their lips still half an inch apart. Both of them looked up at me. "The minstrel let all the animals out before the curse took effect."

"He said," Edwin said quietly, "that you told him to."

"What? Why would I—"

The memory came swift and sudden. I had been running from the spinning wheel, racing to get Rosalin, and I had slammed into the minstrel.

Let the animals go, I had told him. *Twirtle is trapped in his cage. And the dogs . . . Let them out. Please. Just in case . . .*

I gasped, panic and desperation washing over me all over again. And then, in their wake, a sharp stab of loss.

Twirtle was gone.

I could stop looking for him, stop listening for his soft,

rising chirps. Stop being afraid that I would see yellow feathers caught in the thorns. Twirtle was safe. He had flown away before all this happened, into the vast blue sky in the human world. He had lived out his bird's life and died hundreds of years ago.

But to me, it felt like it had just happened.

"Briony!" Rosalin said. "What's going on?" She let go of Varian's hands and rushed across the floor to me. I leaned awkwardly into her, burying my face in her ruffled gown, trying to get my tears under control.

"It's all right," I managed to say through my choked sobs. "It's not . . . It's just . . . It's about my bird. . . ."

But that wasn't really true. I wasn't crying just for myself. I was crying *mostly* for myself, of course, but I was also crying for everyone else in the castle: The ladies. The treasurer. The kennel boy. Everyone who had woken up and realized that someone they loved—that many people they loved—had died years ago and was gone forever.

The horror of it washed over me. I was glad, glad, *glad* the kitchen girls had escaped. To think that, even for a second, I had resented them for leaving! I should have *helped* them leave. I should have . . .

I should have stopped this somehow.

Instead, I had been a part of making it happen.

I have to save Rosalin. Nothing else matters. I had truly believed that, back then.

But I should have been worried for everyone in this castle. Not just my sister.

I sniffled, wiped my nose discreetly on Rosalin's sleeve, and drew back. I looked at them all: Edwin, his brow drawn with concern; Varian, slightly panicked; Rosalin, discovering the snot on her sleeve and giving me an outraged glare.

I couldn't do anything to give the people in this castle their past lives back. But maybe ... maybe ... I could make sure they had a future.

"There's something else," I said as steadily as I could, "that you all should know."

I took a deep breath. I still wasn't sure this was the right thing to do.

But I also wasn't sure anymore why I was keeping this secret. Was it really to protect Rosalin? Maybe part of the reason I wasn't talking was because as long as I was the only one who knew, I was in charge of our story. I wasn't the ignored little sister no one mentioned, I was the one making the decisions. The one saving her sister.

The one this story was really about.

But this wasn't a *story*. It wasn't about only me, or only Rosalin, or only anyone. It was equally about every single person in it.

And who was to say that I was the one who would save us? Maybe someone else would have a better idea. Maybe they would come up with a solution. But they could only do that if they knew everything.

"It's something else the fairy told me," I said. My voice came out thin and small.

Silence. They were all listening, waiting. I took a deep breath, and it hurt going through my chest.

"The fairy told me how to destroy the Thornwood," I said. "I mean, she told me one way to do it."

"Then why," Varian demanded, "did you not tell us before?"

My legs felt quivery, as if I were standing on a window ledge above a terrifying height. "She said the Thornwood will disappear once Rosalin dies in it."

Varian went utterly still, his face drained of color.

Rosalin, too, stood without moving, but her expression didn't change. Her face was grim and resolute.

Of course. She had known for years that this could end in her death. She had known long before this.

I said, "That's not going to *happen*, of course. We won't let it."

"No," Varian agreed. His voice was oddly low, as if he were talking to himself. "No. Not even if it's the only way."

"It's *not* the only way," I said. "The fairy never said it was the *only* way. Just that it's *one* way."

"Did she have any other suggestions?" Rosalin said.

Her voice was cool and calm, completely without expression. I wondered if I was the only one in the room who knew how terrified she was.

"We don't need another plan," Edwin said. "The answer is right in front of us: we accept the fairy's bargain, and then no one has to die."

"We'll be trapped!" I said. My voice was shrill, but I didn't care. "Cut off from the world for the rest of our lives!"

Edwin gave me a faintly apologetic look. "Actually, it's looking pretty good to me in here. Lots of warm, comfortable beds, no one making me work, and now good food, too." He grinned crookedly. "Plus, I like the company. Not at this precise second, perhaps . . ."

I didn't smile back. "You can't think that's enough reason to stay here for the rest of your life!"

Edwin stepped away from me, his smile fading. "You only say that because you don't know what it's like to be cold and hungry."

I couldn't argue with that.

Which didn't mean I couldn't *argue*.

"You won't be cold and hungry," I said. "We'll find a way to make it in the world out there. We'll combine our skills—"

Edwin gave a strangled laugh. "What skills? I've never been good at anything."

"You've never been good at blacksmithing!" I said in exasperation. "That's hardly *anything*."

Edwin shook his head. "You don't understand. I never wanted to be part of some grand tale. I just came here to be safe."

And that, of course, was exactly what the fairy was offering. Safety.

"Rosalin," I said a bit desperately. "You want to spend the rest of your life trapped here? Don't you even *want* to know what the world out there is like now?"

"It's the only way, Briony," Rosalin said. "If we don't put ourselves under my fairy godmother's protection, we're all going to die."

"You don't know that."

"I *do* know that."

"You're acting out of fear. You—"

"You're right! I am!" Rosalin choked on a sob. "Is it so terrible that I don't want to be in constant danger anymore? That I finally have a chance to be safe and I want to take it?"

I looked at the three of them. Edwin was staring at the tips of his shoes like he had only just realized he was wearing them. But Rosalin met my gaze with a regal tilt of her head, her eyes cool.

"This isn't your decision, Briony," she said.

I knew she was right. But I looked past her, at the tables

scattered with leftover food and the chairs knocked over on the floor, and I knew something else.

"No," I said, "it's not my decision. But it's not yours, either."

"Fine," Rosalin said. She crossed her arms over her chest. "We'll take a vote. How about that?"

"Yes," I agreed. "This decision should be made by everyone."

"All right, then." Rosalin cleared her throat. "All in favor of—"

"*Every*one," I said. "Everyone who's part of this. And that includes more than just the four of us."

Varian blinked, and Edwin's head came up sharply. Rosalin looked completely confused.

"There are at least thirty other people in this castle," I said. "Last time, we made a choice that affected all of them, and we didn't even *think* about them."

"We had to!" Rosalin said. "We were—"

"—scared," I finished.

"Yes! We were! *We* were the ones the fairy queen was after! And there wasn't enough time—"

"There's time now," I said. "Whatever we decide, everyone here will have to live with the consequences. So everyone here should get a say."

"She's right," Varian said.

Edwin nodded.

Looking betrayed all over again, Rosalin crossed her arms over her chest and muttered, "I guess I don't have a choice, do I?"

Varian smiled faintly at me. "I think," he said, "you might adjust well to the world outside after all."

"That will be very reassuring," I said, "if we manage to *get* to the world outside." I avoided Rosalin's eyes as I went on. "For now, let's find the rest of the people in this castle and gather them together so we can explain. We should go in pairs, in case we come across part of the Thornwood that's made its way in, or some people who hate us, or . . . well, those are enough reasons, aren't they?"

My voice trembled, and I looked at Rosalin. She was staring resolutely away from me, her jaw tight.

"My sister and I will search the main floor," I said. "The two of you should go upstairs."

I expected Rosalin to object—in fact, that was half the reason I had said it—but she didn't react.

"Good idea. We'll be fine," Varian said firmly. "Don't be afraid."

I bit back my instinctive retort. After all, nobody's perfect.

"Thanks for the advice," I said. "I'll try."

24

It took us a while to track everyone down. As we searched the castle, we saw the Thornwood everywhere. Branches snaked through every window and every crack, clinging to the remaining tapestries with their sharp thorns, breaking through flagstones and knocking over the occasional piece of furniture.

The only place free of them was the royal gardener's workshop, which was the last room we went to. The gardener was sitting at a table by the window, making notations in a ledger, squinting in the moonlight that streamed through the window.

She was a very old woman; I didn't know how old exactly, but in my earliest memory of her, she was yelling at me to get off the rose beds in a high, quavering voice. Rosalin had told me the gardener had that same creaky voice, and the same wrinkled skin, the first time she'd yelled at Rosalin to stop playing with her seed packets.

Her greatest feat—which she talked about on those rare occasions when she wasn't yelling at children to get away from her flowers—was creating roses with alternating pink and blue petals. They were, I had to admit, very pretty.

I waited for her to acknowledge us. When she didn't, I walked across the workshop—a small round room lined with shelves—and looked out the window.

Here, the Thornwood had halted several yards away from the walls. It formed a semicircle around a small patch of dirt that, I remembered, had once been a garden, covered with roses whose various colors and designs depended on the gardener's current ambition. Last I remembered, she'd had her heart set on creating a polka-dotted rose.

Her attempts usually failed—in fact, the blue-and-pink rose was her only success—but in the process of trying, she had filled the garden with a random explosion of colors and scents. It had always been the most beautiful spot in the castle.

Now it was a patch of mud, dark and dank, spotted only with ferns. The air was tinged with warmth and wetness, as if it were spring, but the trees around the patch were all bare branches decorated with thorns—no leaves, no buds, not even any moss.

Inside the castle walls, it was easy to pretend that things were normal, that despite the years we knew had passed, everything was the same. But outside the castle, in that patch of mud, I could see how the years had flown by and left us all behind.

"The flowers couldn't survive," the gardener said without looking up from her ledger. "Too much shade, and those thorn trees draw all the water and nutrients from the ground. My poor roses never stood a chance."

"Don't worry," I said. Too late, I realized that was just as stupid as saying *Don't be afraid*. "We'll plant new flowers once the Thornwood is gone."

Her eyes were small and deep in her wrinkled, papery face, and she was wearing the same grass-stained dress I had always seen her in. "And when, exactly, will that be?"

I looked again at the patch of mud. There were thorn trees sprouting through it near the castle wall, but they weren't nearly as high as the ones around the rest of the castle. Their branches were only clinging to the windowsill; they hadn't even touched the inside walls.

"What are they afraid of?" I said.

"What?" Rosalin said.

"The thorn branches. They're advancing into this

room more slowly than anywhere else in the castle."
There were tiny white crystals scattered along the windowsill. A thin, fragile hope sprang up in me. "Do you keep something in this room that you use to kill weeds?"

"Of course," the gardener said. "My own concoction. A mixture of olive oil, hemlock, and sulfur."

"Where is it?" Rosalin said. "I command you to hand it over!"

I sighed. "If you are willing," I said, "it would be very helpful. We can use it to fight the Thornwood."

"No. You can't." The gardener's jaw clenched. "I've used it all. I threw it out the window. It kept the thorns off for a little while, but . . ."

One of the branches snapped at me. I jumped back and it retreated, scoring a line across the windowsill with one extra-long thorn.

"What's that, then?" I said, pointing to the crystals.

"Salt. I dumped some on the ground, too, to keep the Thornwood from growing." The gardener's shoulders slumped. "That didn't work for long, either. Nothing I've tried has worked. I am sorry, Your Highnesses, but I believe we are doomed."

I took a deep breath. "That's actually what we're here to talk to you about."

The gardener took the news of the fairy's bargain better than most people had, but her expression was extremely dubious. "The fairy queen? Isn't it impossible to defeat her?"

"My sister's fairy godmother *has* defeated her," I said. "Or at least, she kept her asleep for hundreds of years. Even now, the fairy queen must be in a weakened state. Otherwise, she would already have killed us all."

The gardener snorted. "Is this supposed to be an argument *against* my saying we're all doomed?"

"Anyhow," I said, "the vote will be held in the ballroom. If you want to—"

"I'll think about it," she said shortly.

I scurried back to Rosalin's side. My sister edged away from me.

So far, Rosalin had been deep in thought while we searched, speaking only when necessary. I wanted to ask her what she was thinking, but I didn't know where to start.

It wasn't until we were on our way back to the ballroom that she said, "This is a disaster, Briony. And we're handling it all wrong."

Well, that was one place to start.

"Our family has a duty to the people in this castle," Rosalin went on. "We should be protecting them."

"That's what we're doing," I said.

"No it's not! Our subjects don't know any of the things we know. They haven't been in the Thornwood. They haven't spoken to my fairy godmother. They have no way of understanding just how much danger we're all in."

A thorn-covered vine snagged my hair, and I ripped it free. Sharp pain shot through my scalp, bringing tears to my eyes.

"I think," I said, "they probably have *some* sense of it."

Rosalin raised one hand to her shorn hair, then dropped it. "What if they make the wrong decision? Have you even thought about that?"

She was taking such long strides that I had to scurry to catch up. "And you're so sure you know what the right decision is?"

"I trust myself more than I do a random collection of people who don't know what's going on!"

"And you think," I said, "that *we* know what's going on?"

"I think this is our fault, and we need to fix it!"

I stopped walking. I knew my sister, and I knew when she was about to cry.

Rosalin pressed her knuckles to her eyes, took two heaving breaths, and went on. "Our people . . . I wasn't even thinking about them, Briony, when we went to the spinning wheel. I could *feel* the fairy queen reaching for me. I was imagining what it would feel like when she killed me. My fairy godmother told me that the queen is ancient and bored and cruel, that she likes . . . she likes pain . . ."

"Rosalin," I whispered.

"I was so scared, Briony." Now she was crying. "All I could think about was escaping. I wasn't thinking about anyone else."

"Neither was I," I admitted. And though I didn't have all my memories back, I knew it was true. Watching my sister sob with terror, I knew I would do anything to save her; that in the moment when we'd stood together and seen the spinning wheel, I, too, had not been thinking about anyone else.

"No wonder they hate me," Rosalin said. "They should."

"No," I said firmly. "They shouldn't."

Rosalin wrapped her arms around herself.

"That's in the past," I said. "We have to decide what to do *now*. And this time, let's not be the only ones deciding." I tried to smile. "That way, if things go disastrously wrong, at least it won't be entirely our fault."

Rosalin pressed her lips together angrily, and we walked the rest of the way to the ballroom in the silence we should have stuck to in the first place.

———————◆———————

In the ballroom, only two of the tables were filled—one fewer than at the ball. Either we hadn't managed to find everyone, or not everyone had been willing to come. But most of the remaining inhabitants of the castle were waiting around the tables. A few stable boys had chosen to sit near the empty fireplace instead, and the minstrel was strumming his lute while murmuring under his breath, "Princess . . . Blincess? Mincess?"

The gardener stomped in a few minutes later and went to stand in a corner.

Only three members of my father's personal guard were there, but it looked like almost all the squires had come. The kennel boy was scowling darkly; he glanced at Varian and then ignored us. There was also a group of foreign courtiers—Derkholmian, by their dress—who probably hadn't known enough about the curse to get out in time.

They all stayed far from the windows, where the heavy velvet curtains had been shredded to bits. Thorns wove over and around stray bits of fabric, dragging them across the marble floor.

My parents weren't in the ballroom, and neither was the royal wizard. Varian and Edwin had intended to track them down, but when I asked, Edwin shook his head.

"Last anyone heard," he said, "they went with the royal wizard to work on a spell that could save us all. The royal wizard's door was locked, but we could smell incense and hear the chanting from the other end of the hall. Varian and I knocked and shouted as loudly as we could, but they couldn't hear us."

"It's probably just as well," I said, feeling guiltily relieved. "I don't think they would be thrilled with this plan."

"I'm sure they wouldn't be," Rosalin said, "since it's a terrible plan. And also probably treason."

I rolled my eyes and turned to the crowd.

"Ladies and gentlemen of the court!" I cried.

There was no reaction. Everyone continued milling about, talking in low murmurs and picking at the leftover food.

"We have called you here—" I began more loudly, but I was interrupted by a laundress having a coughing fit. One of the guards pounded her on the back until the fit stopped.

Rosalin climbed onto a chair.

"Good people!" she cried. "I beg you to listen to me!"

Instantly, everyone went silent.

Rosalin clasped her hands. Her gown was ripped, her hair was ragged, and thin scratches marked one of her cheeks, but she was still beautiful.

She drew in a breath and choked out, "I am sorry."

I'd *thought* the room was silent before. That was because I hadn't known what true silence sounded like.

"I'm sorry," Rosalin said again. Tears rolled down her cheeks, and her voice shook. "I know you're all here because of my curse and my decisions. My . . . my selfishness. It is too late to change what I did, and I won't ask for your forgiveness. All I will say is that I am truly, terribly sorry."

Everyone underestimated my sister. Even me.

She didn't wait for a reaction. She went on, her voice wavering. "And now you—we—have a choice to make. A terrible choice, but one we must face together."

———————◆———————

It took them an hour to decide. Rosalin, Varian, and I waited outside, trying to determine the significance of the various shouts and phrases that drifted out to us.

"...trapped forever..."

"...enough food..."

"...fairy queen..."

"...impossible to fight..."

"...take a chance..."

We were too busy listening to talk to each other much. Varian and Rosalin sat against the wall at the far end of the entrance hall, his arm around her shoulders. I paced along the same wall, swerving around them every time I passed—which was awkward, but better than walking closer to the thorn branches that now covered the front wall. A few spiny roots had managed to crawl across the room under the rugs; they were discernible only by the curved bumps they made, and by the occasional thorn that pierced the thick wool. As I paced, another thorn pierced the wool, its point gleaming wickedly. The branches on the wall inched closer to us, their thorns packed close together, bristling and sharp.

"We must live free!" someone shouted from inside—it sounded like the kennel boy—and Varian pulled Rosalin closer. I swallowed hard. The people were debating between accepting the fairy's offer or trying to fight their way out. We hadn't told them they had a third option: killing my sister. Nobody had even brought up the idea of telling them.

When the ballroom went silent, Varian and Rosalin got to their feet, holding each other's hands tightly. I went to stand beside them.

Edwin stepped out of the ballroom. He looked at us gravely.

"The people have voted," he said. "They want to fight."

25

That wasn't entirely accurate. The people didn't want to fight, so much as they wanted *us* to fight *for* them. And by *us*, they meant Varian.

The three men of the king's guard did offer their assistance. But Varian shook his head.

"You are brave and strong and true," he told them. "But that means nothing to the fairies. The three of us, who have some connection to our fairy guardian, are the ones who must confront her."

They didn't argue. In fact, they retreated faster than I had ever seen anyone move before.

"*Three* of us?" I said once the guards had gone back to the tables. "What about Edwin? Isn't he coming?"

I didn't have to explain where we were going. *When you decide to accept my offer*, the fairy had said, *come spin for me.* Presumably, we should go to the same place if we were going to reject her offer.

And then—what? Make a new bargain? Take the gold thread and use it to fight the fairy queen on our own?

Neither of those options sounded promising. We were going to have to come up with something different, something smarter. We *needed* Edwin.

"Edwin's been very helpful," Varian said. "But the fairy has never taken notice of him. It's only by coincidence that he's been involved."

"He's the one who found the sword," I said. "He's the one who saved my life. That's not coincidence. He deserves to come with us."

"'Deserves'?" Varian shook his head. "It's not exactly a privilege. Did you notice how relieved the guards were to *not* be included?"

I glanced into the ballroom. Edwin was sitting at one of the tables, between a page and a serving girl. He seemed very busy putting food on his plate. As I watched, he said something to the stable boy sitting across from him, and the boy laughed.

I never wanted to be part of some grand tale.

A thickness rose in my throat. Varian was right. Of course Edwin wouldn't want to come.

"I want to ask him," I said.

Varian shrugged.

I approached the table feeling oddly trepidatious. Considering that we were about to reject a fairy's offer of protection and face her undoubted wrath, the last thing I should have been worried about was whether Edwin would come along. But I couldn't help feeling that if he didn't join us, we didn't stand a chance.

I came up behind him and saw that he wasn't gathering food: he was gathering salt bowls and pouring their contents into an empty wine jug.

My heart leapt. I had told him, before the vote, what the gardener said. "You think it will work?"

Edwin gave me a crooked half-smile. "It's worth a try. Mostly because I can't think of anything else to try."

I forced myself to say "You don't have to come, you know."

His smile vanished. "You don't want me to?"

"No! I *do* want you to. I just—" I stopped. "I just didn't think you would want to."

"*Want* is a strong word." He shrugged. "But . . . do you really think I can help?"

"I know you can," I said.

He took a deep breath. "Then I want to come." He lifted the jug and stood. "Let's go."

◆

The entrance hall was smaller than it had been when we'd left it a few minutes ago. Branches and roots had encroached farther into the castle, not just clinging to the walls but twining through the cracks between the floor's marble squares.

We hugged the interior wall as we passed through the room, staying out of reach of the branches. But once we reached the entrance to the tower, that was no longer an option. Branches had broken through the windows and coiled their thorny way up the stairs, completely blocking the way. I jumped back as one branch snatched at my ankle.

"Varian?" I said shakily. "I think we need your sword."

Varian stepped in front of us and began chopping. He struck at the branches with short, savage motions, and they drew back just long enough for us to get through. Varian's arm moved rhythmically, his breathing coming in swift huffs as he cleared our way and we climbed the stairs. I was so close behind him I kept having to dodge his elbow, and Edwin and Rosalin were pressed just as tightly behind me.

So when Varian stopped short, I rammed into him, slamming my face into his back. I staggered and put a hand out to catch myself, and my palm landed right on a thorn.

I screamed and pulled back, expecting the branches to wrap around my wrist. Instead, they all arced toward the thorn that had pierced my skin. A drop of blood dripped from the thorn's tip, and one of the branches swooped low to catch it. The blood landed on the bark and immediately disappeared, absorbed into the wood.

I curled my fingers around my palm and the agony slicing through it. A drop of blood glistened between my fingertips. I pulled my sleeve hastily over it.

"Varian!" I said. "Keep going!"

Then I saw why he had stopped.

The entrance to the tower room was covered with thorn branches. They crisscrossed and covered the doorway, so thick I could barely see the room on the other side.

Varian lifted the sword over his head. "Stand back—"

A branch snapped from the wall and tore through my sleeve. I pulled away with a shriek, knocking Edwin in the face with my elbow. He yelped and jerked back, bumping into Rosalin, who cried out as she fell. She rolled down a few steps before managing to stop herself.

"Rosalin!" Varian cried, turning toward her. His sword dipped low.

And the thorns attacked.

One branch slammed down on the hilt of Varian's sword, knocking it out of his hand. Another slithered across the stairs at Rosalin and jabbed several sharp thorns into her calf. She screamed, high and terrified, and pulled away. The side of her calf, beneath her shredded stocking, was smeared with blood.

For a moment, the stairwell was completely still. I thought I could hear the branches breathing.

Then they all struck at Rosalin, streaming toward her like they were drawn to the scent of her blood. They shot past me, scraping along the stone, whooshing through the air.

"Stop it!" I screamed. "Get away from her!"

Varian tried to dodge past me and get to Rosalin. I forced myself to look away from my sister and grab his wrist.

"Get the sword!" I said. "Or there's nothing you can do for her!"

Varian looked back helplessly. The sword was held down by vines twined together so thickly they formed a solid mass.

Rosalin screamed again. I let go of Varian.

Then Edwin dashed past us and threw out his hand, throwing a spray of white salt onto the sword.

The vines hissed and shrank away, shriveling as they went. Varian swooped and grabbed the sword hilt.

"The door!" Edwin shouted. "That's almost all the salt I've got!"

He upended the jug over the thorns that were holding Rosalin down.

I couldn't hear them hiss—Rosalin's screams were too loud—but the branches shrank away. Not as completely as they had before, though, and after just a couple of seconds, they shot back.

I lunged for them and grabbed the largest, pulling at it with my bare hands. It could have encircled me easily, but it was too busy trying to get at Rosalin. The bark was rough and slippery, and a thorn scraped painfully against the side of my hand, but I hung on tight, bracing my feet against the stairs. Edwin's hands clamped down next to mine, and with his help I managed to hold the branch still.

Rosalin scrambled to her feet and up the stairs just as Varian cut through the branches covering the door. Through the thin opening he created, I saw the tower room, filled with golden light and completely free of thorn branches.

"Get through!" Varian shouted.

Rosalin hesitated, turning back. "Briony!"

"I'll get her!" Varian said. "I promise! But I need to know that you're safe first!"

Rosalin dashed through the opening. A branch struck out, tearing off the hem of her gown. A pink ruffle fluttered from a thorn as the branches grew back.

Varian slashed through them again.

"You two! Come on!"

Edwin turned. His blue-gray eyes met mine.

"One . . . ," he said. "Two . . ."

"Three," we said together, and at the exact same moment, we let go of the branch and raced up the stairs.

The branches were closing together, faster than before. Edwin dove through. I heard the branches slide against his boots, but then there was a thump on the other side.

"I made it!" he shouted.

A vine coiled around my ankle. I slipped my leg free before it could tighten. "Varian—"

He looked down at me, and his expression froze me. There wasn't a hint of fear on his face. There was something else, something like triumph.

Before I could think about it, he turned and swung the sword again, slicing through the branches. This time, he didn't stop; he chopped again and again, sideways and diagonally, until almost the entire doorway was clear.

The second he stopped, I ran through. I almost wasn't fast enough. A thorn snagged on my hair and pulled several strands out, with a burst of pain that brought new tears to my eyes. I wrenched myself free, into the golden light.

Something was crawling through my hair. I reached up and yanked out a twig. It writhed in my hand, tilting its tiny sharp thorns toward my skin. I threw it at the spinning wheel, and the second it hit the polished wood, it disintegrated into a sprinkle of dust.

I took a few heaving breaths, then turned around.

The doorway was once again covered with thorns. Beyond it, the darkness was so thick that I knew the entire stairway must be covered, too.

There was no way Varian was going to cut through that. The doorway was sealed, and we were trapped.

I took several quick steps to the window and looked down. The branches had grown high enough for me to make out individual thorns.

"My fairy godmother isn't here," Rosalin said shrilly. "How do we make her come?"

I turned away from the window. Rosalin was clutching Varian's hand, and he was looking at her protectively. Edwin had that set, blank expression that I now understood: he was terrified, and hiding it.

"Maybe," he said, "she's not the one you want."

"What are you talking about?" Rosalin demanded.

"Your fairy godmother keeps talking about how to get rid of the Thornwood. But it's not the *Thornwood* we need to defeat, is it? It's the fairy queen herself." He leaned forward. "Maybe we need to find a way to get the *fairy queen* here."

Varian laughed derisively. It would have annoyed me, but I suspected he was scared, too. "And then what? You know the fairy queen can't be defeated. She's far too powerful."

My shoulders tensed. I drew in a breath.

Everyone seemed to agree that it was impossible to defeat the fairy queen. But that wasn't our only option. *It can* trap *the fairy queen,* the fairy godmother had said. And the fairy queen had been trapped once before.

"There's something in this castle," I said, "more powerful than the fairy queen." I looked across the room at the spinning wheel, with its empty bobbin. "She was trapped in this spell, hundreds of years ago, by this spinning wheel. Maybe that's why the fairy keeps wanting us to spin gold thread. She's hinting that we can use it against the queen."

"Why wouldn't she just *tell* you that?" Edwin objected.

"Because she can't. She can't work directly against her queen." I turned to face the center of the room. "All this time, she's been waiting for me—I mean, for us—to figure out how to do it ourselves." *Everything that comes from that spinning wheel repels the Thornwood.* All those hints. "She's been trying to make us realize that the golden thread from this spinning wheel can be used to hold the fairy queen."

We can harness its power and keep you safe.

I started across the room. "So I guess I had better start spinning."

26

I settled myself at the spinning wheel and began to spin.
I spun as fast as I could, pedaling swiftly and steadily,
drawing the imaginary wool in with fumbling fingers. I
was relieved when the wool appeared in my hand, thick
and black; dimly, I heard someone gasp, but I was concentrating too hard to figure out who it was. The pedals
purred smoothly, the wheel whirred, and gold thread
wound thicker and thicker around the bobbin.

"Look," Varian said in a strangled voice.

The thorn branches blocking the door were bulging
inward. One branch broke through and reached into the
room, curving in our direction.

I tried to spin faster and overdid it. Some of the thread
over-twisted and formed clumps, and I felt a sense of dis-
gruntlement from the wheel. I ignored it; I didn't need
this thread to be pretty, I just needed it *spun*. I drew and

pedaled, concentrating fiercely on not letting the thread break. As long as I didn't spin too fast and didn't change the direction of my feet, the thread wouldn't get too thick to jam up the works.

The bobbin was full, so I stopped and started unspooling the thread. The thread was light and slippery in my hand, and made my skin tingle where I touched it.

My life energy had gone into this thread. The thought made me want to fling it away, but instead I held it tighter.

"Your Majesty!" I shouted. "Come and face us! Or are you afraid of a bunch of humans?"

There was a scraping sound behind me. Another branch was snaking over the edge of the windowsill, thorns scratching the stone.

A shudder ran through my body. All the magic thread in the world would do us no good if we couldn't get the fairy queen to come here and be trapped by it.

Unless . . .

I yanked the thread at both ends, twisting sharply, and was relieved when it tore. I pulled it out to both sides and dashed over to Rosalin. Another branch escaped from the door and crawled toward us.

"Turn around," I told Rosalin.

She didn't move, so I started winding the thread around her. Varian pulled his hand free and stepped away, giving me room. He stepped so fast he stumbled, but he righted himself before he fell.

Rosalin grabbed my wrist. "Briony, stop it!"

"They're going to come for you first," I said. "This thread will protect you. I'll spin protection for the rest of us after—"

She shook her head. "You can't spin fast enough. The only way to protect us all is for the Thornwood to vanish, and there's only one way that can happen." Her chin trembled, and she clenched her jaw. "I knew this was going to be necessary when we came here. I'm ready."

The branch touched her foot. Varian chopped it in half with an overhand swing, then whirled and sliced off a second branch that was creeping our way.

Rosalin shuddered but spoke with dreadful calm. "The fairy godmother already gave us the answer. My life powers this spell. If I die, the spell will vanish, and the Thornwood with it. You know as well as I do what has to happen."

"No!" I said. "I know *better* than you do. As usual. We'll get the fairy queen here, and we'll trap her with the golden thread and force her to let everyone go!"

She smiled at me sadly, but the smile looked painted on. "How are you going to get her here?"

"I—I'll think of something."

"I'm sorry I teased you so much. I'll never say anything about your hair again." She did her best to laugh. "Even if *never* only lasts for another few minutes, that's going to be a challenge."

"Stop it!" I wrenched free of her grip and looped a strand of gold around her arm. "Stop being brave! Be scared, and help me figure out how to get the fairy queen here!"

"Take care of Varian," she went on. "Tell him not to feel guilty."

"I will *not*! And Varian can take care of himself!"

Varian was chopping down branches swiftly and me-thodically, and so far, he was keeping ahead of them. But thorn-studded vines were curling over the windowsill and heading across the floor, curving widely to avoid the spinning wheel.

The spinning wheel! Even more than its thread, *it* had power over the Thornwood.

"Come on!" I shouted, and pulled Rosalin to the spin-ning wheel. Edwin joined us immediately. The thorns hissed in our direction but didn't come closer.

Varian screamed. The sword flew out of his hand and landed on the floor. He lunged for it, but a branch shot in front of him and he pulled back.

Within seconds, the sword had been covered by a writhing mass of thorny vines.

Edwin gasped. "What happened to them not being able to touch it?"

He was still clutching the jug of salt, but it was empty. What else could we use? Sulfur, the gardener had said, and hemlock. That didn't help. The sword was the only thing that could cut through the Thornwood, and it was gone. . . .

Something nudged the edge of my mind, a shadow of an idea. Before I could grab it, Varian screamed and fell to his knees.

Rosalin ran to him, right into the thorns. They jabbed at her, but weakly—they seemed to flinch back from the gold thread—and she was able to grab Varian's hand and drag him toward the spinning wheel, wrenching herself free of the thorns that sank into her skin.

As soon as she was close enough, I threw the rest of the gold fibers over her head. Then I hopped back onto the spinning wheel. I began spinning again, pumping as hard as I could. The thread spun out, agonizingly slowly.

"It's not going to be enough," Varian gasped. He was holding his side. "They're too strong now. They were able to take the sword from me. . . ." He gasped, a pained gurgle, and hunched over, clutching his side.

The branches arced above us and met overhead in a harsh series of scratches and cracks. Thorns and twigs rained down on us. One scraped the side of my hand.

Another landed in my hair, catching in its tangles and tugging them down.

Varian threw his body over Rosalin, pushing her to the ground. A few thorns hit him, too, then skittered across the floor.

I spun and spun and spun. The wheel whirled, so fast it was a blur. The gold thread spooled out, not fast enough.

Rosalin wriggled out from under Varian. He grabbed for her, but he was too slow, hindered by his injury.

The thorns hissed at Rosalin, then drew back.

"It's the thread," Varian gasped. "It's keeping them away."

I tried to pump harder, but my breath was coming in harsh, dry gasps, and I slowed down despite myself. Rosalin grabbed the thread tangled around her and started pulling it over her head.

"Rosalin!" I screamed. *"Don't!"*

"It needs my blood," Rosalin sobbed. "Once it has it, you'll be free. You'll all be safe." She yanked a tangled mass of gold over her head. "Name your first child after me."

"I won't!" I shouted. "I hate the name Rosalin! So you had better live, and name your *own* child after yourself!"

Rosalin tore the last of the thread off and thrust both hands into the thorns. Their hiss rose around us, sharp and sibilant and triumphant.

I jabbed my palm into the spindle of the spinning wheel.

It hurt. It *really* hurt. For one blinding second, the pain was all there was. Then I blinked out tears and saw that the thorns had drawn back even farther, leaving a larger space around the spinning wheel than they had before. My blood had given the spinning wheel power.

Varian stared at me, his eyes bright with sudden hope. "Your blood works against the Thornwood, too," he whispered.

I couldn't respond. My hand hurt so much that it was all I could do to keep spinning.

And I wasn't sure how much longer I could manage that.

Varian pointed at the spinning wheel. Its surface was clean and polished; the wood had absorbed my blood so fast there was no longer a trace of it. "Briony! You share your sister's blood. The Thornwood will take *you* instead of Rosalin!"

I almost forgot the pain in my hand. I turned to look at him. That wasn't hope in his eyes, it was—

"What are you saying?" Rosalin demanded. Her voice cracked. "That I should let them take my *sister*?"

Varian looked at her. Whatever expression had been in his eyes, it was gone.

"Of course not," he said. "I'm sorry. But I can't . . ." He stopped. His voice shook. "I can't bear to lose you, Rosalin. Not when I just found you. I . . . I love you."

Rosalin stared at him, eyes wide. He swallowed hard and reached for her hand. She stepped closer to him.

This time, the kissing *was* gross.

"Um," Edwin said. He stepped closer to the spinning wheel and watched them with an expression that was probably very similar to mine. "Does it really seem like the best time for this?"

"I wouldn't have thought so," I gasped. Sweat dripped into my eyes, but I didn't want to stop spinning long enough to wipe it away. *This* thread, strengthened by my blood, would be even more powerful. Though it wouldn't do us much good unless we could get the fairy queen here. "Nobody's asking me, though."

"Maybe it will help?" Edwin suggested, after several awkward seconds had passed. "I mean, it seems like kissing puts a stop to this spell . . . at least sometimes. . . ."

I stopped spinning. I turned to stare at Rosalin and Varlan. This kiss was taking a lot longer than their first one.

Their first one.

Which I had also seen. Because I had been woken before the kiss. Because . . .

You're the important one, the fairy had said.

She had been lying. She had known it was what I wanted to hear, so she had known I would believe it.

But it wasn't true.

This was the thought that had been nudging me earlier. Varian had hidden the sword before he even walked into my sister's room. Definitely before he kissed her. Yet Edwin had seen him do it.

Because I wasn't the only one who had been woken before the kiss.

Which meant it hadn't been the *kiss* that broke the curse.

The fairy had told me as much. Another hint that I had missed. *Your sister kept trying to wake up.*

So what had it been? If Rosalin had woken herself up, why did we even need a prince?

I stood perfectly still, remembering with crystal clarity the fairy's words: *The one who calls himself a prince has already found her.*

"Edwin," I gasped, turning to him. "Take over the spinning for me. Quickly!"

"What?" He blinked several times. "I—I don't know how—"

"You don't need to know how," I said. "Not with this spinning wheel. *Now,* Edwin!"

He nodded.

I slid off the stool. In the moment before Edwin took my place and got his feet on the pedals, I grabbed the new thread—the one spun with my blood—and yanked it free. It was just long enough for me to stretch my arms wide and hold it taut.

Rosalin and Varian finally broke apart as I approached them. Around us, the branches hissed and shook. One snagged in my hair, and I jerked myself loose.

"No, Briony!" Rosalin said. "I won't let you sacrifice yourself."

"That's not what I'm doing." I faced the writhing branches and pulled the thread tight. My hand throbbed dully.

"That won't work," Varian warned. The gleam I had seen earlier was back in his eye.

"It's magic thread," I said. "Spun not only with my strength, but with my blood. It will hold off the Thornwood."

I turned and stepped toward Rosalin, thread held high. But I wasn't looking at her. I was looking at Varian, seeing him through new eyes, filtered by what I should have realized the moment the fairy flew me over the woods and showed me that the Thornwood didn't surround the castle. That the Thornwood was all there *was*.

No one, no prince, no savior, had come to us through the Thornwood.

He had come *from* it.

Rosalin flinched and ducked, right before I whirled.

Varian blinked at me. That was all he had time for before I brought the thread down over his head and around his neck. I crisscrossed the ends and pulled them, making a noose that tightened against his throat.

"And it will also hold a fairy," I said. "Isn't that true, *Your Majesty?*"

27

Varian threw his head back and laughed.

As he did, he changed. His body shimmered; his face lengthened; his eyes grew larger. Two wings, blacker than black, snapped shut over his shoulder blades.

He didn't look like a woman, but he wasn't a man, either. He was a creature. A *being*. A center of power.

Memories flashed through me.

The one who calls himself a prince.

The Thornwood belongs to the fairy queen.

The thorn branches pouncing on the sword. It wasn't the *sword* they had been avoiding all this time. It was the person holding it.

And the fairy vanishing every time Varian entered a room. Saving us only after he tried to abandon Rosalin to the thorns. Offering her bargain while he lay unconscious ...

And then vanishing again in the second before he woke.

That poison had been meant for Varian after all. The *fairy godmother* had poisoned him. Her. So that she could appear at the ball.

I cannot appear in the presence of my queen, not after defying her like this.

"Varian?" Rosalin whispered.

The fairy queen smiled at her. "My love. Won't you throw yourself on those thorn branches? For me?"

Rosalin shrank back. I tightened my grip on the gold thread.

My love. My heart ached for my sister, but I kept my focus on the creature I had trapped.

"That's why you pretended to be her prince," I said. I was inches from the fairy queen, and there was so much power on her face, so much cold hatred, that I had to fight the urge to step back. The malevolence in her eyes was not at all hidden now. "Because in order for fairies to use our blood, our sacrifice has to be voluntary. You wanted Rosalin to fall in love with you so she would agree to *die* for you!"

The fairy queen laughed. She no longer looked at all like Varian. There was nothing human left in her face—her eyes were yellow slits, her mouth a gash across her too-white skin.

"You humans have so much energy," she said. "So much strength that we can put to good use. But you have to give it to us willingly. Which means we have to spin stories to convince you to do it." She kept her gaze on Rosalin. "All I needed was your life, freely given, and I could have freed myself from the trap my ungrateful subject set for me. I could have taken revenge on her and regained my throne. It's a disappointment, really, how little you were willing to sacrifice for true love."

"But you saved me!" Rosalin said. She backed away, her eyes wide and pleading. "*You* saved me from the Thornwood! Why?"

"Because your death *then* would have accomplished nothing. I needed you to *volunteer* to die. To sacrifice yourself willingly." The fairy queen smiled, and her smile stretched so wide it wrapped around the sides of her face. "Everything I did, Princess, was designed to make you love me. The guise of a prince. The trickery with the sword—which was never a magic blade, by the way. I found it on the floor of the guard room and made sure that wretched boy saw me hide it."

And then used it to save me from the Thornwood—but all the sword had done, in Edwin's hand, was cut through and damage the branches. When Varian had swung it, they had disintegrated into dust. Yet we had still believed it was the sword, and not Varian himself, that the trees were afraid of.

"I did everything I could to fit myself into the story your fairy *godmother* concocted. To make you believe I was the prince, to make you fall in love with me, to make you willing to sacrifice your life for me. And it almost worked, didn't it?" She turned to me, her eyes glittering. "It would have worked. If not for you."

I forced myself not to loosen my grip on the gold thread.

"You humans so love to tell yourself stories, and *her* story had a prince and true love at the end. It was working. Every time I saved her, every time I confessed a supposed truth to her, she fell in love with me a little more. It's *your* fault she didn't agree to sacrifice herself for my sake." That sentence was a snarl, and it froze me like I was a hunted animal. "You and your doubts and your accusations. You agreed to keep my supposed secret, but you wouldn't believe in me the way you were supposed to. You can't imagine how often I wanted to wring your neck."

My palms were sweaty, and my finger cramped painfully around the thread.

"I said as much to Rosalin. I thought she hated you, too. She certainly complained about you enough. But oh, you should have seen her! Prickly as a porcupine!

How dare I attack her little sister!" She laughed again. "And then I realized who, exactly, Rosalin would agree to sacrifice herself for."

Rosalin looked from me to the fairy queen and back. She made a low, whimpering sound.

"It was so easy," the fairy queen said, "to get you to put yourself at the center of the danger. You so wanted to believe that you were important."

I swallowed. "The fairy godmother said—"

"She wanted you to believe you were important, too. She thought you might be more willing to fight me than your sister would be. If she'd had her way, *you* would be the heroine of this tale." She leaned forward. Her voice went soft and compelling. "And you still can be. I will let you free, *just* you, to go out into the world and tell of your escape. You can shape this story however you like. All you have to do is let me go."

She didn't get it. She still didn't.

But now I knew one important thing: the golden thread really worked. The fairy queen was trapped. She needed *me* to let her go.

Which meant I had something to bargain with.

"Promise," I said, "that you won't hurt us. And then I'll consider—"

She reached out and grabbed me by the throat.

Her hands were long and thin, bony and strong. She

lifted me from the floor, and I couldn't breathe. I tried to scream, and I couldn't do that, either. Panic filled me as I struggled to draw air into my lungs and no air came.

I wasn't even aware of letting go of the thread.

I thudded to the ground and took several gasping, painful breaths. The last breaths, I knew, that I would ever take.

But nothing happened.

I looked up and saw, through blurry eyes, that Rosalin had pulled her mass of golden thread over the queen. She held the queen in its tangled mesh, and Edwin held it by its other side.

The fairy queen hissed—a sound exactly like the one the thorn branches made—and struck at Rosalin. Rosalin stood her ground, and the queen's hand stopped, a thin claw, inches from Rosalin's throat.

My heart climbed up my chest in desperate, frantic beats. I ran to where Edwin stood, grabbed the thread from him, and shoved him in the direction of the spinning wheel.

The fairy queen snarled in frustration, her face inches from Rosalin's. But still she didn't touch her.

I drew in a breath, suddenly realizing what was stopping her.

You agreed to keep my supposed secret.

But I hadn't *just* agreed. I had demanded something from her in return.

Swear to me that you won't hurt her, or I'll tell her the truth.

"You can't hurt her," I said.

The fairy queen gnashed her teeth at me. Her teeth were pointed now, as sharp as the thorns, and there were still too many of them. Behind me, I heard the whir of the wheel as Edwin began to spin.

"Fairies have to keep their bargains," I said. "When you were pretending to be Varian, I agreed to keep your secret—your *fake* secret. In return, you promised you wouldn't hurt Rosalin."

The fairy queen whirled on me.

"If you hurt me," I said quickly, "that will count as hurting her."

"You don't even like each other!"

"That is not the point!" I pulled the thread harder. "You don't understand humans. You don't understand *families*. But I think you know I'm telling the truth."

The fairy queen's face twisted. But in her anger, I saw that she did, at last, know. Even if she would never understand.

"All right," she spat. "Let me go, and I'll give you back your castle. I'll give you back your world."

"And you won't hurt us," I said. "You won't even *try* to hurt us."

"Agreed."

I stared at her, trying to see the trick, and she smiled. It was a perfectly human smile, which looked terrifying on her completely inhuman face. "Fairies always keep their bargains, child. Don't you want this to finally be over?"

I looked at Rosalin, and then at Edwin, who was pedaling frantically. I looked at the fairy queen, and her glittering smile made terror arc through me, the same panic I'd felt hundreds of years ago when I'd seen a fairy for the very first time.

But I had a lot of experience, now, with being afraid. I knew how it could make you forget about everything and everyone else.

And I knew that it didn't have to.

"By *us*," I said, "I mean humans. *All* humans. We'll set you free, but you can't hurt any of us, ever again."

She gnashed her teeth. I pulled the golden net tighter.

"*Agreed*," she snarled. "Let me go."

It was too late to wonder if I had made a mistake. I let the golden thread fall to the ground, and Rosalin did the same.

The fairy queen struggled with it for a frantic moment before throwing it off. It landed in the branches of the Thornwood, which shrank and crumpled, disintegrating into bits of bark.

The fairy queen straightened. Her wings spread, so large they covered the entire space that was free of thorns. She glared down at me, her eyes old and yellow and cruel, showing no trace at all of the man—the disguise—she had called Varian.

Then she vanished.

The thorn branches vanished, too. They didn't crumple, they didn't disintegrate; it was as if they had never been there. The room was round and airy, and sun streamed through the window, filling the chamber with golden light.

I went straight to Rosalin. She was standing with one hand pressed to her mouth and the other to her stomach, staring at the spot where the queen had been.

"I'm sorry," I said. "I know you thought you loved him. But he never really existed, Rosalin. He was just a disguise the fairy queen invented. You haven't lost anything—"

"Oh, be quiet!" Rosalin said. "You don't know the first thing about it. You're just a child."

I had been raising my arms to hug her. I let them drop. "Just a child? Then why was *I* the one who—"

"Really," the fairy godmother said. "This is very disappointing."

Rosalin and I whirled. The fairy stood in the corner of the room, arms folded over her chest, one foot tapping the floor. Her wings caught the sunlight and cast shimmering color across the walls.

"I noticed," she said, "that you didn't make her promise not to harm *me*."

"No," I said. "I didn't." I crossed my own arms. "Do you expect a reward for dragging us into this?"

"I suppose not. Humans are *so* ungrateful." She sighed. "I had grown fond of you, you know. And I did save your life once or twice. Does that count for nothing? Do you want the queen to kill me?"

"She hasn't killed you yet," I said. "And you managed to beat her once before."

"That doesn't mean I can do it again."

"It means," I said firmly, "that it has nothing to do with us. Keep us out of it from now on."

"Oh, so now *you* expect a reward?" She smiled at me, her too-wide mouth stretching wider than ever, and then she vanished.

I didn't much like that smile, but I didn't have time to think about it. I heard a rattling moan behind me and realized it was Edwin. He was hunched over the spinning wheel, pedaling frantically, sweat making his face shiny. His breath came in frantic gasps.

"Oh, right," I said. "You can stop spinning."

He stopped immediately, and the wheel ground to a halt. I looked at the bobbin. There was new golden thread wrapped around it; the spinning wheel, apparently, still worked.

"I thought it was probably safe to stop," Edwin managed to say between pants. "But I didn't want to take any chances, not until both fairies were gone." He slid off the stool and groaned. "I twisted something in my back. Not," he added quickly, "that it wasn't worth it."

His spinning hadn't actually accomplished anything. I had told him to spin just to get him out of the way. But this didn't seem like the right time to mention that.

I turned to Rosalin. She was already heading for the window, her face bright in the sunlight, tears streaking her cheeks.

Edwin and I hurried to join her.

Below us, the land stretched to the horizon in a sweeping vista of hills and trees. The forest faded into mountain peaks, so darkly green they seemed almost gray, with roads running through them like tiny strips of steel.

Something drew a sharp line across the sky, and I tensed. *Fairy godmother,* I thought—but it was something different, small and sleek and gray with triangular wings. It pulled the clouds after it in a long, thin line.

"What *is* that?" I said.

Edwin gave a small, delighted laugh. "I suspect we'll be saying that a lot over the next few days."

I looked at him and smiled, and he met my eyes and smiled back. On the other side of me, Rosalin took my hand—luckily, the one I hadn't stabbed with a spindle. I could feel excitement or fear—or both—thrumming through her. Clearly, the world out there was far, far different from anything we could even imagine.

None of us had any idea what we would find when we finally walked out the castle doors.

I guessed it was time to find out.

➤ EPILOGUE ➤

There have been a lot of stories told about my sister, I know. Most of them are available at the castle bookstore. They sell very well, even though you'd think the tourists already *know* the story. Otherwise, why would they be here? Entrance tickets to the castle are not exactly cheap.

I mean, yes, the purple polka-dotted roses are very popular, and so are Rosalin's cakes. Plus, we have signed copies of the royal wizard's bestselling book, *Inner Magic: How I Found the Courage to Break the Rules of Sorcery and Discover My True Power.*

But you don't have to come here for that. We ship worldwide.

None of the stories mention me. But I'm okay with that. Let Rosalin be the one the tourists bother, badgering her to take photos with them and making copies of her gowns to wear to costume parties. Rosalin claims she doesn't like it—she says she's devoted to her new passion for baking—but Rosalin says a lot of things these days. She claims she's only "putting up" with the agents who want her to be a model or an actress. She says the photography and film classes she takes are just for fun, that she doesn't want to make a career out of them. And—most ridiculous of all—she claims that she only "likes" the electrician who has been modernizing the castle, and she's "not interested in getting serious with anyone right now."

I mean, she's already kissed him more times than she kissed Varian, back when she thought he was her destined husband. Does that sound not serious?

Rosalin's pretty sensitive on the subject, though. All I did was politely point out how much time she was spending with him, and she went on a twenty-minute rampage. We were out in town at the time, too. Not very good for our image.

So I've let it go. It's not like I don't have enough to keep me busy. Running the castle is time-consuming, even with the treasurer and the ladies-in-waiting helping out. Plus I have to lead a number of the tours, which is exhausting; you wouldn't believe the questions I have to answer. (My least favorite: "So who are you, again?")

Luckily, Darella—that's one of my sister's ladies-in-waiting—has turned out to be a genius at organization. She does *all* the birthday parties, arranges the court minstrel's "reunion tours," and handles the complaints from the people who are disappointed by the royal wizard's magic show. In return, I smooth things over when my parents are rude to "the commoners" (it's taking them a while to adjust).

On top of all that, I have to deal with this thing called "school," which . . . well, I'm not even going to get into that. Let's just say that sometimes, I wish I were still trapped in the castle.

Point is, I'm busy. And when I *do* have time to sit down and write, my letters to Edwin always seem to take priority. They're important: he needs someone to keep him grounded, now that he goes to that fancy school for geniuses.

He (mostly) hasn't let the school go to his head. And he hasn't forgotten who his friends are, either. Last time he came home, he bought me a parakeet. Chirpy doesn't sing, but he's a beautiful shade of light green, and he's really, really smart. My friends from school (okay, fine, school isn't all bad) are always begging me to bring him to class and let him be the class pet. We'll see.

All of this is to explain why it's taken me so long to write this story down.

Rosalin doesn't understand why I've bothered. She says it will just be one of dozens of books, and nobody will be able to tell that it's the truth.

She's probably right. But I have no plan to publish this account. Like I said, there are plenty of others. And there will be more; I'm told that the kennel boy and two of the ladies-in-waiting are busy writing their own.

And in the end, does it really matter who they tell the story about?

Rosalin has always known she was the center of a tale. To her, that was what made her special. I don't need that. I can let her have her story.

Well. Unless she goes back on her promise to never criticize my hair again.

In that case, I'm going to tell the whole world.

Acknowledgments

So much gratitude!

To Diana Peterfreund, for reasons too numerous to list.

To Jodi Meadows, for teaching me and my daughter how to spin. Thank you for all your helpful comments, both spinning-related and plot-related. Any SWSOs (Spinning Wheel–Shaped Objects) that remain in this book are entirely the fault of the author.

To Stephanie Burgis, for insightful critiques, and for calm answers to unnecessarily panicked emails.

To my invaluable critique partners: Tova Suslovich, Christine Amsden, Elizabeth Lazear, Sima Braunstein, Michael Greenhut, Sol Kim Bentley, Nancy Lambert, Merrie Haskell, Victoria Rothenberg, Aryeh Breitstein, Seth Z. Herman, Erin Cashman (it's been a long time in the trenches together!), and Day al-Mohammed (both for your helpful critiques and for inviting me to the writing session during which I found myself, to my surprise, finishing the book).

To my even more invaluable young readers: my

daughters, Shoshana and Hadassah, for allowing me to use them as test-drivers for this book (and for help with kingdom names); Shlomo Sheril; and Bella Kotek.

To my husband, Aaron, for everything and for always.

To my parents, Jacob and Esther Suslovich, and my in-laws, Ray and Sandy Cypess.

To my agent extraordinaire, Andrea Somberg, for this book and for all the other books.

To Wendy Loggia, for thinking this book was great when she first saw it, and then helping me make it actually great.

To Ali Romig, for coming in just in time to make a difference. I'm so glad I get to work with you!

To Carol Ly and Kelsey Eng. As I'm writing this, I haven't even seen the final version of the cover yet, but I can say with absolute confidence that I'm going to love it. I keep the preliminary sketches on my phone so I can glance at them while I revise.

To all the incredible people at Delacorte Press, including Colleen Fellingham, Tamar Schwartz, and everyone else I haven't met yet—I'm looking forward to when I do! I'm excited to be part of your team.

And last but not least, to the staff at the Kosher Pastry Oven, where at least 50 percent of this book was written. I'm glad to finally have an answer to "So, when is that book you're working on going to get published?"

About the Author

Leah Cypess is the author of four YA novels: *Mistwood, Nightspell, Death Sworn,* and *Death Marked.* Both *Mistwood* and *Death Sworn* were on the *Kirkus Reviews* Best Books for Teens list, and *Death Sworn* was a *Teen Vogue* Most Exciting YA Book of the Year. She lives in Silver Spring, Maryland. *Thornwood* is her middle-grade debut.

leahcypess.com